Paper Boats

An Anthology of Short Stories about Journeys to Australia

Yaşar Duyal

Compiling Editor

Foreword by Alice Pung

CAMBRIDGE
UNIVERSITY PRESS

CAMBRIDGE UNIVERSITY PRESS
Cambridge, New York, Melbourne, Madrid, Cape Town,
Singapore, São Paulo, Delhi, Mexico City

Cambridge University Press
477 Williamstown Road, Port Melbourne, VIC 3207, Australia

www.cambridge.edu.au
Information on this title: www.cambridge.org/9781107608887

First published 2012

Cover design by Kerry Cooke
Typeset by Kerry Cooke
Printed in China by C & C Offset Printing Co. Ltd

*A Cataloguing-in-Publication entry is available from the
catalogue of the National Library of Australia at* www.nla.gov.au

ISBN 978-1-107-60888-7 Paperback

*15% of net sales of this book will be donated to a girls' school in Afghanistan
with the aid and assistance of the Afghan Red Crescent Society.
http://arcs.org.af/en*

To my father, Ahmet, a real hero and inspiration to me, and to my mother, Kiymet, who has been a true survivor all her life

Acknowledgements

For all the wonderful people who believed in this project at Narre Warren South P-12 College, for his invaluable support and encouragement right from the start to the end, Principal Mr. Rob Casamento, for her tireless work with the students, Multicultural Education Aide Ms. Farhnaz Zamani, and for his help in class with the students, VCE ESL teacher Mr. George Theodorou. Finally, to my patient wife, Serren, and our two beautiful daughters, Tayla and Tarim, for putting up with the extra work at home.

- Yaşar Duyal

I would like to thank the following people for their contribution in the development of this book: Judith Ridge (Westwords), Loralee McKenna, Anne Bell (Underdale High School), Sally Wilson (Findon High School), Dede Putra for the illustrations and the staff at Cambridge University Press, especially Isabelle Sinclair.

To Yaşar, thank you for your enthusiasm and your tireless dedication to this project.

A special thanks to Alice Pung for generously donating her time and effort in writing a brilliant foreword, along with her unwavering support for this very special book.

And finally, to the talented authors for allowing us to publish your amazing stories. This book is for all of you.

- Margie Dela Cruz (Publisher)

Contents

Foreword

"It is always sad when someone leaves home, unless they are simply going around the corner and will return in a few minutes with ice-cream sandwiches."
– Lemony Snicket, *Horseradish: Bitter Truths You Can't Avoid*

Lemony Snicket started writing his hugely successful and popular book series about three orphaned children who experience progressively worse events after the death of their parents and the burning of their home at around the same time that the real-life events of the narrators in *Paper Boats* was taking place. My younger sisters grew up with Snicket's books, and they were awesome entertainment, allowing children all over the world to feel empathy for the plight of three hapless kids who were at the peril of their fates.

The stories in *Paper Boats* are extraordinary because they concern real-life events just as dangerous, vivid and unfortunate as Snicket's novels; and they are narrated by voices of great insight, humour and fortitude. Fatima Moradi writes movingly of being born twice, Kpana Bolay was a witness to unspeakable horrors. Syed Hussain Mosawi, Mohammad Mohsim Jafari and Jaweed Rahimi set sail alone to Australia to escape oppressive regimes. Sayed Hayatullah Mosawi, Zahra Ali and the protagonist in Izel Öztürk's story survive a leaky boat and detention. Jamila Shirzad shows great resilience as a nine-year-old girl with a sprained ankle escaping the military.

Yet there is hope in the darkness. Taiyeba Ansari writes movingly of surviving post-traumatic stress and finding faith through her depression. Blaise Mupenzi David speaks of his love for soccer games, Kpana Bolay discovers the compassion of a good teacher, and Maisam Haidari finds a new beginning. Robert Matyus discovers dancing, while Kobra Moradi expresses the secret joy of knowing the power of the pen for the first time, and aspirations of meeting Michael Jackson. Nazifa Reza discovers a place of belonging. Melissa Miller and Azaara Perakath's narrator discover the stoicism of their grandmothers and mothers, while Roshan Jafari discovers his voice and Nilofer Zafari discovers the vast beauty of Western Australia.

These stories cover great tracts of land, space and time; they extend to war zones all over the world, but the voices share some common traits: they are brave, raw and life-affirming. Perhaps one day the authors will buy ice-cream sandwiches for their own children, and talk about how they once were writers and came from a place far away. But even if they don't, they are all survivors with unassailable spirit.

- Alice Pung

About the foreword author

Alice Pung is a writer, lawyer and teacher. She was born in Footscray and grew up in Braybrook, attending local primary and secondary schools in the Western suburbs.

The author of *Her Father's Daughter* and *Unpolished Gem* and the editor of *Growing up Asian in Australia*, Alice has received enormous critical acclaim for her writing. *Unpolished Gem* won the 2007 Australian Newcomer of the Year award in the Australian Book Industry Awards and was shortlisted for several other awards, including the Victorian Premier's Literary Awards, the New South Wales Premier's Literary Awards and *The Age* Book of the Year 2007. *Unpolished Gem* has been translated into other languages and is also published in the UK and US.

She has had stories and articles published in *Good Weekend*, *Meanjin*, *The Monthly*, *The Age*, *The Best Australian Stories 2007* and *Etchings*.

In 2008, Alice was the Asialink writer-in-residence at Peking University, and in 2009, the Australian representative at the Iowa International Writing Program. In 2011, Alice was the Australian representative to the US Department of State 'Fall and Recovery' writers' tour of disaster and conflict sites of America. She has also given guest lectures at Brown University, Vassar College, Peking University, the University of Bologna, the University of Milano and the University of Pisa.

Alice has worked extensively with both primary and secondary school students through 'Booked Out', and is currently the writer-in-residence at Janet Clarke Hall, the University of Melbourne. She has a deep passion and empathy for youth issues, and believes in the power of good humour (and not-so-good puns) to help surmount adversity.

A qualified legal practitioner, she currently works part time in the area of minimum wages. The rest of her time she devotes to writing and school visits.

Introduction

It all started on the train on an excursion with my students at the end of 2009.

That day, I was moved hearing about the dreadful journeys and the traumas the students had gone through at such a young age, just so that they could have some kind of normal life. It felt like the first time I read about my father's last words during the war; like hearing about my mother and her parents' experiences as refugees in North Cyprus in 1936. Those words hurt but they inspired. So, the idea for the collection was born.

The collection aims to provide, for the very first time, a rare but very critical window of opportunity for these young students, mostly from refugee backgrounds, to have a louder voice and share the stories of their journeys to Australia. What is also critical is for other young people to hear, appreciate and get to know these voices. This will no doubt make it easier for such students from refugee backgrounds to settle in at school and in other environments, holding their heads up with pride and building a better life.

The authentic nature of each non-fiction story gives life to the collection. Hence, the stories are powerful in resonating with real-life people and places and delivering significant messages for us all.

The writer Kimberly Ridley said 'When we let our stories flow, we can astonish and renew each other.' I hope the stories in this collection also flow into the minds and hearts of all the people who read them. I just wanted the students to know that their stories matter. They matter.

- Yaşar Duyal

About the compiling editor

Yaşar Duyal migrated to Australia in August 1993 from the Turkish Republic of Northern Cyprus. He worked first as an education aide supporting children with learning disabilities at Springvale Primary School. Since then, he has taught Studies of Society and Education (SOSE), English, English as a Second Language (ESL) and English Literature at Westall Secondary College, Minaret College, Parkdale Secondary College, Eumemmerring Senior College and Narre Warren South P-12 College. Yaşar is currently the Head of English and teaches English Literature and VCE English at Highvale Secondary College, Glen Waverley. Since 1994, Yaşar has also been teaching and coordinating the study of Turkish Language at the Victorian School of Languages and Western Thrace Turkish School in Keysborough and has been a chief assessor for VCE Turkish. He has established an English Language Centre for international students at Parkdale Secondary College and has been an English/English as an additional language leader at Narre Warren South P-12 College. Yaşar has worked with many students and parents from refugee backgrounds over the years. The programs he helped set up for refugee mothers and students at Narre Warren South P-12 College were recognised by the Governor's Award for Excellence in Multicultural Education in 2009. In December 2011, he received an award for his community service in education in multicultural Victoria from the Victorian Multicultural Commission. Yaşar is currently completing his PhD studies in Education at the University of Melbourne.

A Daughter's Story
Fatima Moradi

I was born twice.

The first time was as a baby girl in Afghanistan in 1994. The second time was as a teenager when I landed at Sydney airport in 2005.

Seeing my father after almost six years was the most unforgettable memory of my life. When he left Afghanistan sometime in 1999, my mother and I had to go and live with my uncle's family. Even though we had my uncle's support, Mum had to provide for her children. When I think of those times, I see her sitting behind the sewing machine, making dresses so that she could support her seven children. At night she worked by candlelight.

Looking after seven children without a man's help may seem like an easy thing to do in a Western country, but it is not easy in a country that is governed by the Taliban. Women had no rights. They were not allowed to work or have control of their lives. They could not leave the house without a man. If they did, they would be punished severely or even shot.

Like most Afghanis, my mother dreamed of having a baby boy. She gave birth to five girls before her dream came true. My dad, on the other hand, didn't care so long as the children were healthy. Every time Mum gave birth to a girl she got upset. Dad just asked if the baby had both legs, both arms, and looked like any other child. He was grateful for that.

I was Dad's favourite. Before my brother came along, Dad used to say, 'If I don't have a son I have my daughter Fatima. I wouldn't replace her for 10 boys'.

I will remember that sentence until I die.

My sister was born in 1995. A rocket hit our house when she was two or three months old. That's when my parents realised that life in Kabul was impossible.

We decided to move to a place called Jaghori, which is in Ghazni province. Even though it is only seven or eight hours drive, it took us almost a year to get to the village. That's how hard it is to travel in a war zone. It just isn't safe. We stayed at family or friends' houses for some weeks or even months until it was a bit safer to travel. Then we'd move on and stay with someone else for a while. Finally, we arrived in Jaghori.

It wasn't easy for Mum and Dad to forget the happy life they had in Kabul. But they had to move on and accept the fact that life has its ups and downs and the world doesn't always remain the same. My dad was the manager of a hotel in Kabul, and we had the best and most comfortable life that anyone can imagine. It was a different story in Jaghori. In the country, people had to work for their own food, and almost everything else they needed. The women looked after the house and cared for the sheep, cows and goats. The men farmed and some of them travelled abroad to countries like Iran or Pakistan to make extra money. We lived with my uncle for some years, until Dad decided it was time to make a better life for his family.

Dad left for Pakistan sometime in 1999. My younger sister was one or two months old when he went away. Living away from Dad was hard. I missed him a great deal. But having a woman as strong and amazing as my mother around the house meant we had nothing to worry about.

Mum is a fighter. You have to be when you move from one place to another and have to take care of seven children almost on your own. The good thing was that she had the support of her brothers. They were very generous, allowing us to live with them and their extended families. After all we've been through, I love them like my own family.

My father came to Australia in 2000. I wonder if he would have done it if he knew that getting the Australian government to accept his refugee status was harder than the dangerous journey in a rickety old boat. To make things harder, Osama bin Laden attacked America in 2001. This made things doubly difficult for refugees from Muslim countries. The crazy thing was that while many Afghanis feared the Taliban and were terrified of being killed in the war, the world was suddenly scared of Islam and Muslims. But the thing is, we had no choice. We either stayed at home and got killed or risked a dangerous journey in search of a better life. It took almost two years for my father to get settled in Australia, and it took us about three years to get the news from him. By that stage, we didn't even know if he was alive or dead. Can you imagine what that is like?

My mother decided to moved back to Kabul when Hamid Karzai became president of Afghanistan in 2001. By that stage, our house was nothing like we remembered. Everything was stolen: the carpets, the curtains, desks, tables and cupboards. Even some of the doors were missing. Kabul had become a very ugly place. There were hardly any houses left standing. And you couldn't possibly live in the ones that were still upright. Walls were peppered with bullet holes. Every family had lost a loved one. For my family it was my 25-year-old cousin, Ahmad, and my aunt's husband.

Mum still talks about Ahmad and how he was shot dead on the way home from the tailor, where he went to get his wedding suit. Everything was ready, Mum says. Ahmad was getting married, everyone was happy, and then they heard the Taliban had shot him. At least we know what happened to him. My aunt's husband went missing, and we never heard from him again.

Everyone had a story to tell about how loved ones were killed or missing. Some had seen their loved ones get shot or blown up by bombs. The streets were packed with children and adults without limbs, begging. Yet, in the middle of all this, we were happy to be back in our country. The hope was that our beautiful Afghanistan would become the heavenly country it was before the war, a place where people lived in peace and harmony.

Dad finally decided to bring us to Australia in 2004. I'm not sure why he waited that long to bring us here. But since he is religious, I thought part of the reason was that he didn't want us to grow up away from our own culture, religion and people.

I was on top of the world when I heard that we were going to Australia. I made a big list of things I would do: get educated and find a good job were high on that list. I also thought I would always wear my Afghan clothes and stick to my own culture. I planned to always listen to my parents and do as they wish, and to always do my prayers. There was

A Daughter's Story

a lot of other stuff. But things changed when I came here. I realised that things never go the way you want them to. You have to make sacrifices in order to fit in.

We left Kabul in 2004 and went to Pakistan. Was I sad? The answer is no. Maybe it's because I was too young to understand the cost and sacrifices I would have to make in order to live in a country that is totally different to my own. All I wanted was to get to Australia and see my dad. We stayed in Pakistan for almost a year before the Australian embassy in Pakistan interviewed us.

That was the most amazing year of my life. I got to know my dad's side of the family for the first time. I had lots of cousins, uncles and aunties I had never met. We were total strangers to them and they were total strangers to us. Even my mother didn't know most of them. One year is not long enough to get to know your relatives, but I was glad we got to know them a little. That's the story for a lot of Afghanis. You have cousins that you never knew existed. Three decades of war separated every Afghani family from their relatives and friends. The war left millions of us homeless, and forced us to spread all over the world like stars.

Our visas came through in December 2005. We came to Australia and settled in a town called Griffith. For the first few weeks we just relaxed and got to know our father again. It wasn't until school started that I realised life here wasn't going to be easy.

My first day in Year 7 had to be the worst day of my life. I didn't know the language, and the students made fun of me. In one of the classes the teacher told one of the students to take off his hat. He said he wouldn't do it until my sister took off her headscarf. I wasn't wearing a scarf, but when we were walking home some of the students ran after us and pulled my sister's scarf off.

The scarf wasn't the only problem. We wore different clothes; we ate different food; we had a different lifestyle … Everything was different about us. To make things easier, I mixed a little bit of Afghani with Aussie culture. That made both parties happier, but we were still living between two worlds. As time passed, life got easier. I made friends at school. Just as

I settled in, my sister finished Year 12, and we had to move to Melbourne so she could go to university.

Life is easier in Melbourne. It is a very multicultural city compared to Griffith. I made friends here quickly, but I still miss the friends I made in Griffith and I'm glad we keep in touch. We have lived here for almost two years, but I'm still not used to the weather. Whenever I go out I don't know what to wear because the seasons change so much in one day. I live my life a little differently to the way some other Afghanis live. For instance, I don't wear a headscarf; I don't hang out with Afghanis at school; I go to parties; I go shopping. But I do have my amazing Afghani friends outside school. All of these girls mean the world to me, and I will never forget the happy times we've had together, no matter where life takes us.

Some people judge a book by its cover. They think I am a bad girl because I don't wear a headscarf. But that doesn't matter to me. All that matters is my family's opinion. So long as I have their love and trust nothing matters. They know I won't do anything against their will. That gives me energy and makes my life happy. I couldn't ask for anything more.

A Daughter's Story

The Space In Between
Kpana Bolay

My name is Nowa and I have a story to tell.

I was born in Liberia, the youngest daughter of an influential family. My father's name is Toimu and my mother's name is Korlu. I had seven sisters and three brothers. This made for a very busy home. My oldest sister Miata has a daughter who is the same age as me. Zoe is my niece, but she is also my best friend. Life was always happy until the war came. Now my family is broken. Some are dead for sure and some I am uncertain about. My name is Nowa – it means 'the space in between' in Kpelle, like a space one would seek to hide.

Liberia was a wonderful place until the war began. My home country was a caring environment but, when the war broke out in Monrovia, it became a harmful place – a place to fear. Terrorists and rebels rule with cruelty and violence. Children are forced into killing and working for the political cause that is financed by blood diamonds. People had to leave their homes and shelter in the forest, under bridges or anywhere that was away from the fighting.

I have lived like this, clutching at my nanna's skirts for security; there was never a safe place. When the war started, I, along with my parents, my nanna, my uncle, my brothers and sisters and, of course, my best friend Zoe escaped into the forest. We were there for a long time. I slept on the ground and lived on fruits from the trees. Zoe and I clung to each other many times, wondering if we would live to see another day. We managed for about three years while the rebels were overthrowing our town.

Hiding from the rebels was hard. Many men dressed as women and lived in silence. It was important to survive. Rebels raided when they learned that there were people living in the forest, and the people moved on if they wanted to survive.

One time, Zoe and I became separated from our family. We cowered, shaking, praying for our lives, and by the grace of God the hilarious face of my father dressed as a woman peered at me through the dense undergrowth. Silently, he clasped my hand and Zoe's and we were reunited. If it hadn't been such a serious a situation, it would have been the funniest thing to see.

The rebels penetrated further into the forest and people began heading for another country. I followed my family, Zoe at my side; we were women of the world at 10 years of age. Our family was lucky. We were still all together. My father at the front, with my uncle and my beloved nanna: my mother, my sisters and brothers, Zoe and me following.

A journey to where? Zoe and I discussed this at length. All we knew was that we must stay alert and follow instructions. Many, many kilometres of walking and while walking you had to listen to the sounds of guns, carefully trying to work out where the sound was coming from, how far away it was.

There was fear everywhere, on everyone's face. For me and Zoe, confusion and pain were constant companions. The jungle insects preyed on our soft skin. Sores developed where we scratched, blisters and splinters filled our feet. My nanna soothed me with her voice; even though she was tired, she rocked me in her arms.

Without warning, gunfire exploded around my head. I looked for my father and uncle. The ear-splitting screams of my sister, Zoe's mother, pierced the thick jungle air. A bullet had penetrated her leg, leaving her shinbone smashed and splintered. It bled heavily. I sat frozen, watching my mother hurriedly drag her into the cover of the foliage. She wrapped a frayed cloth over the pulsing wound and begged her to be silent.

From our hiding place we watched the rebels kick the lifeless body of someone from our group. We hadn't even noticed that she had paid the ultimate price for freedom.

Soon I realised that it was my beloved nanna, lying not far from us, being abused by the rebels. Rage welled in my 10-year-old body. My mother covered my mouth with her free hand to stop me from crying out. My shoulders heaved with great sobs. We stayed there for hours, waiting for safety.

My father, my uncle, my brothers and sisters were nowhere to be seen. From our hiding place, we watched as the rebels committed acts of complete horror. They tortured men. They killed them in front of their loved ones for fun.

The Space In Between

I felt vomit gushing to my mouth, but I was unable to spit it out for fear of making a sound.

I feared sound as it meant certain death. We would certainly be killed and I believe that the Lord Almighty saved us by giving us the strength to be silent. As quickly as they had arrived, the rebels left.

I was as stunned as my mother, sister and Zoe.

We were separated from the rest of the family. We prayed that they had survived.

Had my father and the others been shot too? 'Please Lord, spare them', I prayed.

My mother insisted that we keep moving. I was brave and ventured to find something that could be used as a walking aid for my sister. I did not cry because I knew that if I cried I might be heard.

I was creeping through the jungle in search of a suitable branch when someone grabbed me from behind. My heart stopped and in that moment I believed that I was to be attacked and have unspeakable injustices committed against me. I had seen the rebels do it to other young girls. Then I realised it was my uncle. His harsh grip loosened into a warm hug as he lifted me up. He kissed me gently on the cheek and I knew that we were going to be safe.

I followed my uncle to a small, roughly constructed hut, deeper in the jungle, while my father fetched my sister, Zoe and my mother. Only one of my sisters and one of my brothers squatted out the front of the hut, kicking at the jungle floor. Once we were together again the horror of what had happened became apparent.

One of my brothers was dead. Another could not be found. We prayed. Two of my sisters were dead, three could not be found. Again we prayed.

We ate our food raw that night, as we had on many nights, so that the smoke from the fire could not be seen. During the night my father and mother planned what to do next. It was decided that we would travel to Sierra Leone and seek help. How that help would come I didn't understand.

My father explained that we could be refugees and seek asylum in a country far far away.

'Astrilia?' I could hardly say it.

Many others in our group had talked about this place, but I never imagined that I would live anywhere else but my beloved Liberia.

I spent five years in a Sierra Leone refugee camp and all the while I prayed for my brothers and sisters lost to the civil war. I prayed to be reunited with them.

My family and I were subjected to interviews and health checks. Many questions were hard and I didn't know the answer. I worried that I had been a bad daughter and shamed my family.

We changed our names to Western ones so that we would be accepted in this new country. My father chose the name James, but the authorities didn't believe my father was who he said he was. We had no official papers to prove our identities. He went back to his real name, Toimu. They still didn't believe that he was our real father.

Just when it seemed that we would never leave, my father received a letter of acceptance to immigrate to Australia.

'What about my brothers and sisters?' I cried.

My mother wept and my father was broken. Confusion and conflict surrounded us again.

Our country had been ravaged by war; whole villages had been wiped out. Unspeakable crimes had been committed and it was still not safe to return to Liberia. We couldn't live in this refugee camp forever. Our family was fractured. Hope is all we had.

We were no longer the lucky family.

My name is Nowa and I have a story to tell.

I arrived in Australia early one Thursday morning in 2007. I was 15 years old. When I arrived I knew nothing about my new country, nor did I know anyone who lived here.

It was winter. It was really cold and I wished I hadn't come. As time has passed, though, I have become used to it. I am slowly making

The Space In Between

connections and figuring out the way things are done. At first, I couldn't even work out where to buy food or where a store was. Over time, I learned to read and even write, and I feel lucky to be an Australian citizen.

I am faced with the challenge of figuring out what the future holds for me. It is my dream to become somebody and make a change in the world. I believe that as long as I have a vision I will be able to fulfil my dreams.

I want to find my brothers and sisters. I want everyone to practise tolerance, to respect each other's religion and culture, and I want to be truthful but not hurtful.

Life is always changing and I want to always look forward.

My name is Nowa. It means 'the space in between' in Kpelle. It is like an emotional bridge between Liberia and Australia, just like the heart between the two lungs or a child in between a parent's arms.

My name is Nowa, and I have a message. My message is one of peace.

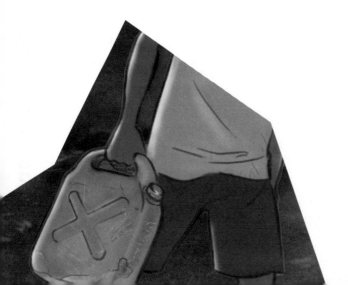

Jadwiga
Melissa Miller

My grandmother told me many stories about her past.

Jadwiga Zusko was born in March 1936, in Kopryn, Poland. Jadwiga's mother, Ewa Zusko, separated from Jadwiga's father and later married Eugenusz Budner. He left for World War II in 1939, leaving a stepdaughter, stepson and wife alone.

One cold night, Russian soldiers came and took Jadwiga and her mother Ewa from their farmhouse, leaving behind Jadwiga's older brother Wasyl, who was visiting his grandparents, Tekla and Teadow Tereszczuk. Ewa was not allowed to fetch Wasyl or her parents, so the boy was left in the village with his grandparents.

The soldiers took Jadwiga and Ewa to a local school. They were then forced to board a livestock train, which took them to another village in Poland. The village was on the edge of a forest and Ewa worked among the trees for a long time, collecting mushrooms and firewood.

Jadwiga was left alone while her mother worked. She was three years old – not even tall enough to see through the only window in the room. Still she cared for herself, eating, sleeping and keeping herself occupied during the day. Jadwiga was too young to know what was going on. But she knew something was wrong. Her brother Wasyl had always been her protector. The thought of him not being there to take care of her was very upsetting.

Later, Jadwiga and Ewa were placed in another livestock train and taken to a ship. It took them to Uganda in East Africa. When they got there they went to the Polish Refugee Settlement run by the English government. Accommodation was very basic; two families of the same number of people shared one room.

Late in 1943 they learned that Nazi soldiers killed Jadwiga's grandmother Tekla. She was 53 years of age.

The following year, Eugenusz Budner, who was serving under British command, was killed at Monte Cassino on the Italian front.

Jadwiga went to school in Africa and received a good education. Ewa was a stay-at-home mother, relying on her late husband's small pension. They were very poor. Jadwiga used to dress an onion with cloth and pretend it was a doll. One day, while Jadwiga was out, a young boy with a knife came and started teasing her about the doll. He told Jadwiga he was going to cut off its head. He tried. There was a scuffle and he accidentally cut Jadwiga's hand.

Jadwiga had many friends. Some moved to other countries, some passed away at a young age and others disappeared without a trace. But it wasn't all horrible. During this time she learned to speak Russian and basic English. She also learned to cook traditional Polish food by watching her mother.

One day, while out walking with her friends, Jadwiga found a dead crocodile. This was not uncommon. They started to play with it and Jadwiga said it was one of the best days of her life.

Jadwiga was left alone for a year while her mother went into hospital to recover from tuberculosis. When Ewa returned home, they travelled through the jungle to buy chickens and eggs from the local Africans. Sometimes the locals came to the refugee camp to sell fish.

The Polish Refugee Settlement was disbanded in 1950. The residents were told to choose another country to move to. Out of the many choices, Ewa chose England. They arrived there in 1950, five years after the war in Europe ended. Soon after, Ewa had a relapse of tuberculosis and spent two years in hospital. Jadwiga went to boarding school.

Jadwiga worked in a number of jobs. First she was a part-time helper in a fish and chip shop. Later, she did sewing and made rhinestone jewellery. She found it very difficult to find and hold a job because her English was not good.

When Jadwiga was 16 she married a boy she had known in Africa. His name was Eugieniusz Wiechec. Eugieniusz worked in the Cadbury chocolate factory. Altogether the couple had five children, three girls and two boys. They all lived in Birmingham.

Jadwiga's beloved brother Wasyl had survived the war in Europe and moved to Russia, where he married and had two children. During the Korean War he served with the Russian forces. After being shot in 1955, he developed gangrene and lost both his legs. He retired soon after.

Early in 1968, when Jadwiga's youngest child was nearly seven, Jadwiga and Eugieniusz decided to move to Australia. The Wiechec family caught the ship the *Fair Star*. The trip took four or five weeks. After arriving, the family stayed in Melbourne for two weeks. They then moved to Matraville in Sydney for 18 months. Eugieniusz worked at a car factory and Jadwiga worked at a childcare centre.

Eugieniusz knew a Polish family in Adelaide that offered them accommodation until they found a place of their own. The family moved there and Adelaide became their permanent home.

In those early years, they were so poor that they used suitcases for tables and chairs. Jadwiga worked jobs in various factories before finding work as a full-time night shift worker for Clipsal, trimming plastic moulds, until she was forced to give up work because of ill health.

Ewa was still living in England. In 1970 she applied to the Home Office for a visiting visa for Wasyl. The visa was refused. The reason given was that he might not go back to Russia. At that stage Wasyl was a widower with two children aged seven and 12. He was also disabled. Ewa was very upset about not being able to bring her son to England. She had not seen him for 30 years and she was not getting younger. She was heartbroken when Wasyl died two years later, especially as she was unable to find out why. Russian authorities denied her medical information.

In early 1983, Ewa applied for a visa to come to Australia so she could be with Jadwiga. Her application was refused because Ewa had tuberculosis. An Australian consultant suggested she get more information about her case and try again. But, sadly, she passed away in 1984. She never saw her daughter Jadwiga again.

Jadwiga's brother-in-law, Janek, was of great help to the family. As he still lived in England, he organised Ewa's funeral and death certificate, and communicated with the family in Australia.

Jadwiga

Jadwiga still lives in Adelaide. Wasyl's children occasionally write to her, but no one in the family can read Russian. She is old now but her memory about the early years is sharp as ever. She tells her life story as a refugee and as a young girl growing up during the war as if it happened yesterday. It is unbelievable that she can remember so much.

A Daughter's Story

Research and Discussion

1   Life was unbearable under the strict rule of the Taliban in Afghanistan. Find out about life under Taliban and sharia law in Afghanistan and compare it to life and law in Australia.

2   Do you believe women will ever have equal rights in Afghanistan? Why? What steps should be taken to achieve this? Explain by giving examples from the story as well as from your own life.

3   Fatima says it is a mystery to her why it took her dad a long time to sponsor his family to come to Australia. Use the clues provided in the story to solve this mystery and explain why it would have taken her father that long to sponsor them. In your answer, consider the important events, their consequences and Australian refugee policy during the time her father escaped on a boat to come to Australia.

Writing and Creating

1   Refugees escape their countries for a variety of reasons. They experience difficult times in their own countries and later in the countries they seek refuge in. Make a list of the difficulties refugees may experience when they come to live in Australia. Use examples from 'A Daughter's Story' to help you. Share your list with others in class.

2   Fatima said, 'we were still living between two worlds' when describing her feelings about living in Australia. In a paragraph, explain what she meant by this. Use examples from the story to help you.

3   Put yourself in Fatima's shoes and write a diary entry describing your feelings and an event that could take place in your life if you and your family were to start living in Afghanistan.

The Space In Between

Research and Discussion

1   Nowa, her family and her best friend Zoe are all running away from the rebels in Liberia. Research and find information about this war. What kind of war is it? How did it start and who are the sides? What are blood diamonds?

2   People were being killed mercilessly in the forest. In order to survive the war, many people went into hiding in the forests and some men, like Nowa's dad, dressed like women. What other strengths and survival skills did Nowa and others have to display to survive when they were on the run? Use examples from the story to support your responses.

3   During their time in the forest Nowa and her friend Zoe witnessed many unspeakable acts of violence and killing committed against innocent people, including women and children. Can there ever be a war where no innocent people suffer? Explain your answer with examples.

Writing and Creating

1   Draw a map and mark some current wars in the world as well as statistics on the casualties, refugees and child soldiers forced to fight in these wars.

2   A simile is a figure of speech that involves comparing one thing with another thing of a different kind, mostly using words such as 'like', 'seem' and 'as'. Nowa's name means 'the space in between'. Find examples of the similes she uses at the end of her story to describe herself and use these in a paragraph to explain the meaning of the story's title. Find the meaning and the background of your name and share it with the class.

3   At the end of her story, Nowa expresses her wishes about tolerance, respect, truthfulness and hope. Draw a table and provide examples from everyday life for each of Nowa's wishes. For example, write how someone may show respect for another person's religion or how they show tolerance towards another person or culture.

Jadwiga

Research and Discussion

1   'Jadwiga' is a story that takes place during World War II. Research, using the internet, why Ewa's country Poland was involved in this war. Who were the Allies fighting? Explain why the Russian soldiers might have taken away Ewa and Jadwiga in the story.

2   What were the disadvantages of living in Africa for Ewa and her family? Were there any advantages at all for Ewa and her family living in the refugee camp in Uganda? Explain by giving examples from the story.

3   Explain the relationship between war, hope and family by giving examples from the story 'Jadwiga'. Start by finding their definitions first.

Writing and Creating

1   Draw a table to compare and contrast the life of refugees during World War II and today.

2   Melissa tells the story in third person. This is only one way of narrating a story. Discuss other ways of narrating a story in class. Choose a part of the story, change the narrator to first person and rewrite it with Jadwiga as narrator.

3   Refugee camps, broken families and loss are some of the many consequences of war. What other consequences of war can you think of? Make a list and share it with others in class.

4   Draw a character chart and explain what happened to each character at the end of the story. Comment on whether they were able to achieve happiness.

My Mother, My Hero
Kobra Moradi

I was born during a time of uncertainty. The first sounds that echoed their way through my ears were the loud and daring sounds of bomb blasts, along with the feelings of woe and grief. This was the case for many children born in Afghanistan during the civil war.

Born in a country where many females have limited rights, I had few opportunities of having a bright future. This is how it was for hundreds of girls like me. Women in Afghanistan had very limited rights and opportunities to hold on to.

But in the past years, Afghanistan has been moving forward. People are starting to realise that in order for Afghanistan to be a sustainable country, it needs to give its women the rights to take part in economic, social and political life. In today's Afghanistan, many of the teachers, doctors, politicians and activists are women. Afghanistan might not be the best place for women to thrive, but there is a hope …

Three or four months after I was born, my family moved from Kabul to Jaghori, in Hazarajat. We lived there, in the midst of poverty and segregation, for seven years. Life was hard. It was difficult for my family because my dad was away and we did not know anything about his safety or survival. My mum sewed clothes and sold them in order to take care of her children. When I think about my mum in those days, I see a brave woman and a hero who did her job very well, despite the fact that she was taking care of seven children in a country where there was little support for women. She has been an inspiration and a motivation to me. Looking at my mum and other brave women of my country, I can say that a man may be physically stronger or more powerful than a woman, but a woman is emotionally resilient and can endure terrible pain.

After years of living without my father, we received news that he was alive and safe in a country called Australia. We did not know what Australia was or where it might be. One of my siblings thought it was like Hazarajat, mountainous and isolated.

When my uncle told my mum about my dad, she dropped to her knees and cried. I did not know whether they were tears of happiness or hope, or maybe both. For my siblings and I, Australia was a new hope, a

wonderland where we could study, experience the wider world, interact with different people and learn new things.

We decided to go back to Kabul. The entire family walked through the mountains for endless cold nights. We were hungry, exhausted, thirsty and terrified. Each time someone stopped us, my mum hid all her children under her big *chador*. Even though our feet were swollen and we were dehydrated and hungry, we continued to push ourselves. With each step I reminded myself that we were getting closer to my dad. I could feel safety. It was near and yet so far … With each step, my gloomy heart lit up with joy.

At last, we arrived in Kabul. It was February 2001. We all held hands and looked around, confused about where to go. After Jaghori, the streets of Kabul were busy. Beggars were everywhere, some without arms or legs. They hummed words of sympathy and assistance, but no one paid attention. Maybe people were too selfish, or they had heard and seen too much pain and had become desensitised. Everyone was minding their own business: shoemakers were polishing shoes, shopkeepers were chanting slogans and advertising their products, buyers were bargaining, the poor were begging and the children ran around like desperate birds that have been let out of their cage.

A week later, my siblings and I were enrolled in a school. The first time I held a pen I immediately pictured myself sitting in an office and writing notes. As I examined my book and my pen more carefully, I thought of stories that I could write in my new book. I could not stop smiling.

As people looked forward to what 2004 would bring for them, we made our way to the city of Quetta in Pakistan. Our visas came through a year later. We said our goodbyes to our relatives at the Peshawar Airport and got on the plane. When we were on board, I showed my little brother a little dot and told him that it was Australia.

We arrived in Australia on 14 December 2005. The simplest things seemed incredibly clever and unimaginable at the time. One of these was the fact that doors opened and closed without me touching them.

I remember thinking: 'There are ghosts in Australia. Maybe we should move to another country'.

Life in Australia has been an amazing experience. I am very thankful to Australia for giving me the chance to live, the opportunity to study and make my own future, and more importantly, the chance to see a smile on my mum's face. Australia has taught me what it means to be kind and loving. Today I am very proud to say that whilst I am a Hazaragi girl from Afghanistan, I am an Australian as well.

After finishing my studies, I hope to work hard with different people and help those who are in need.

Being a victim of poverty and racism, and a witness of historical persecution, I know how it feels to be so desperate and in need of kindness. I know how traumatic and aching it is to be displaced and misplaced as a refugee. Uncertain of your future, uncertain of whether you are going to make it to safety alive, uncertain of whether you will ever see your family happy … Uncertainty – an agonising pain that grips every refugee by the throat. I am really looking forward to the day where every child in the world gets an equal chance at a better life.

My Mother, My Hero

My Name is Fatima
Jamila Shirzad

I knew that my parents wanted to leave Afghanistan when I was nine years old. They had been planning it for a while. They wanted a fresh start, away from the havoc in that country. They couldn't take it anymore; the Taliban had killed my grandparents and my mother's 12-year-old sister. My parents said that if the Taliban weren't there my sister Khadija would go to school.

One night they told my three-year-old brother Hussain to be very quiet and that we were moving to another place. We could not wake up our neighbours.

My parents had found a man who could give us a ride to Pakistan. If we were caught we would all be dead. There were seven people, plus luggage, in a five-seater car. It was not pleasant. I had my own seat but my sister had to sit on my dad's lap and my brother sat on my mum's lap. There were no seat belts.

We stopped at the border. The men got out of the car and talked to policemen with guns in their hands. Two policemen came over and made sure we weren't carrying anything illegal. Then they shook hands with the men from the car and that's when I saw that the driver had bribed the police officers. Money had exchanged hands. I kept this to myself and did not say a word to anyone. It was a taboo subject, even among the family.

When we got to Pakistan we stayed in a hotel room. It was really shoddy but we put up with it. I was starting to enjoy myself when one day I heard my parents say that we were still not safe and that Australia was accepting refugees. There were two ways to get there: by aeroplane or by boat.

Only Australian citizens could go by plane. So really there was only one option for us: to go by boat. But that was very risky.

My dad was a bricklayer. It was really bad for his back and I wished I were a boy so that I could help him. I hated seeing him come home late at night and go to work early in the morning. He was in his late thirties, but he looked like he was in his late forties.

He managed to raise enough money to buy five aeroplane tickets to Malaysia. It was my first time in a plane and I was very excited. But I was the only happy one. My sister was airsick. My brother's ears hurt. And my parents were worried about their sick children.

In Malaysia we slept outside for one week before my father met a man who could help us. He spoke Farsi (our mother tongue) and he helped my dad find a dealer to change our Pakistani money to Malaysian currency. He also helped us find a hotel room. My dad invited him to stay with us, but the man said that he already had a place and that he had been living there for about a year. He told us that he wanted to go to Australia too, and that he had found a man who could take him by boat. My dad asked who this man was and he said that he was a prisoner and that he and others had paid him a lot of money and also bailed him out of jail. My dad said that we wanted to do the same thing and asked whether we could join them. The man was not sure and said it would be really tricky because there were a lot of us and we might get caught. My dad said that he would pay more money – 5000 Malaysian ringgit. The man agreed.

Two weeks later we got into a car and drove to the boat. It was small, with many people waiting to get on board. I was praying it did not sink. We boarded and sailed away. But we didn't get very far.

Four vessels surrounded the boat. It was the Malaysian military. We were taken to prison. It was the most horrible feeling I ever had. The prison guards gave us dirty looks and treated us like animals. I felt sorry for my little brother. Imagine a three-year-old kid in jail. The food was bad and always tasted horrible. We slept on rugs on the floor.

One day the people who shared our cell bribed a guard to buy us a handsaw and paint the same shade of black as the bars on the windows. The guard bought the stuff. During the night, the men sawed through the bars and then painted over them to fool the guards. When they finished there was a hole big enough for a person to crawl through. Ropes were made out of torn sheets.

A fit guy went out the window first, then the children, followed by the women and the rest of the men. My poor mother looked really pale when she stood on solid ground. When we were all gathered, we ran to a nearby forest. It was pouring with rain. I slipped and sprained my ankle. I did not tell anyone because I thought they would get angry with me. I was part limping and part running. Every time I put pressure on my foot it felt like I was going to faint. I couldn't breathe properly. My mum noticed, but I told her that it was nothing.

Eventually we made it to three waiting vans. Everyone packed into them and they drove off. I can't really remember where we stayed after that. My foot had swollen and I was in a lot of pain. A little while later a man told us he had found a ship captain who was willing to take us to Australia.

We snuck onto the boat and set off. It was rough weather and many people got sick. People were praying and reading the Qur'an.

The whole time I was in the boat I felt I like I was in a trance. Everything was like a dream. When we finally got close to the Australian coast, a navy ship came along and took us to Christmas Island. After a lot of interviews and many sleepless nights when we thought we were going to be sent back, my family was accepted. They took us to Western Australia.

Finally, I had a country to call home.

The Never-Ending Journey
Syed Hussain Mosawi

I was 15 years old and alone when I set out to gamble with life. The voyage from Afghanistan to Australia could either reward my family or torment us with eternal pain.

On the way to Karachi in Pakistan, the bus stopped so that passengers could go for evening prayers in a mosque. Two Hazara men stayed behind. I found out why soon enough.

I entered the mosque and started to pray. That's when I noticed that everyone was staring me with infinite hatred. My heart was beating fast and I became very afraid. I rushed back to the bus as soon as I finished. I thought that praying with open hands, the way Shia Muslims do, was either a really daring thing to do or a big mistake.

It was almost midnight when the bus stopped at a security checkpoint. A policeman entered the bus and did a routine search. Then he approached the two Hazara men who hadn't got off the bus and started slapping them. Not because they didn't pray, but because they were Hazara. He really got stuck into them and no one did anything to stop him – not that anyone could. Everyone was too afraid. I felt like a criminal.

Our only crime was that we were different. We were discriminated against even though we all believed in one religion, one God, one Mohammad and one Qur'an. However, we were still treated worse than criminals for having our own Hazara identity.

While I was at a hotel in Karachi, the television news showed dozens of dead bodies. They were all Hazaras who had been trying to go illegally to Iran. They died trying to find a better life. Precious human lives lost. Like all the other Hazaras who were leaving Pakistan, they had hopes of a better life after the sacrifice of leaving their loved ones behind. Look how they ended up.

After more struggles we ended up in Malaysia.

I was placed in a small hotel room with 30 other Hazaras. There was no food and no way to get it. I slept on the ground in a sitting position. Days passed. One night I saw a truck with a container waiting outside the building. It was going to take us to the shore. The instant I saw the container, I wondered if that's how those other Hazaras had died.

Around 50 people joined us. A man told us to get into the container and, since we had no option, we did as we were told. The door closed with a loud bang and it was time to leave. Nobody knew where we were going. Our eyes waited for the moment when the doors opened to let us out. It was dark and warm in there. After a while it became hard to breathe.

I stayed optimistic, but everyone else was counting the seconds.

The doors opened after 45 minutes. Everyone got out. The joy of being in a new place, with hopes for a better and safer future, was too much. After almost two hours waiting in a factory, we were told to go down to the harbour.

On arrival, I saw a small boat filled with people. They were pleading with us not to get on. I was among more than 20 people who refused to get in the boat. It was small and overloaded and it would have sunk. Another container took us back to the hotel. Getting into yet another black, airless container didn't bother me so much this time. I was too tired.

The next day we heard that Indonesian police had arrested the people on the boat. We felt lucky.

Our next chance came two days later. Once again we were driven in a container down to the harbour. Another boat was waiting. This one didn't have so many people in it, so we boarded. But it wasn't to be. The minute everyone got in, the Malaysian police showed up and arrested us.

We were locked up and left to wait. Time passed. A police officer suddenly came in and started beating up people. He slapped a man really hard and hit someone else with a thick piece of wood. I was so afraid my heart was pounding in my chest.

That night we slept on the cold, hard ground, not knowing what was going to happen to us. I remember being able to smell fish.

The next morning, without explanation, we were set free. Once again everyone was happy. But I didn't know what to think. My chances of making it to Australia were looking slim.

That night we boarded a boat that was big enough to carry around 78 people. Hungry and thirsty, we sailed for five nights. The men in charge had told us that the boat would arrive in Australian waters on the eighth night. Everyone eagerly counted down the days.

Unfortunately, within reach of our destination, the engine stopped working. Stranded in the middle of the ocean, I could see the disappointment in people's faces. Many cried. Somehow we managed to get close to a beautiful island and we stayed there until a mechanic came to fix the engine. Then we were on our own again.

The sun was very warm during the day. It was hard to be in the same place, seeing nothing around you but water, feeling like you weren't moving anywhere. At night the temperature dropped and countless stars came out, which was amazing.

Two days went by. One morning the Australian Navy intercepted the boat. It was a red-letter day – a day of good luck – for everyone but we were still afraid of being sent back. Each second was like an hour.

We spent 14 days on the navy ship and then we were transferred to Christmas Island.

I spent three months in the detention centre there, waiting to find out if I got my visa. It was a very tense time.

It finally came through and I was so happy. I thought coming to Australia would fix everything. I dreamed of a peaceful life with my family. My first and last wish was to have them with me. I suffered a lot on that journey, but I was happy knowing I was doing it all for their sake.

In August 2011, I found out that my younger brother died in Pakistan. He had gone out for morning prayer on Eid Day. A car bomb exploded outside, claiming dozens of lives. People said the explosion was so powerful that windows broke kilometres away. My brother's shattered remains were sent back to my mother.

I don't know what lies ahead for me in this life, but I feel like my journey is not yet over.

The Never-Ending Journey

My Mother, My Hero

Research and Discussion

1   The author describes Australia as 'a new hope' and 'a wonderland'. How did coming to Australia benefit the author and her siblings? Provide examples and evidence from the story.

2   At the start of her story, the author says she was born during a time of uncertainty. Do children born in Afghanistan today face similar conditions? How is this different from children born in Australia? Is this fair? Share your opinion and ideas with others in class.

3   'Born in a country where many females have limited rights, I had few opportunities of having a bright future.' Use the information in the story to explain the above statement in relation to women's rights in Afghanistan and in Australia.

Writing and Creating

1   a   Use your dictionary to find the meaning of the words 'limited', 'segregation', 'resilient', 'isolated', 'opportunities', 'desensitised', 'activists', and 'displaced' and write them in your book.

    b   Using these three word classes, noun, adjective and verb, classify these same words in a table.

    c   Write one sentence using each word.

2   Reread the part where Kobra and her family arrive in Kabul in February 2001. Use the descriptions and the information provided in this part to draw the city life in Kabul. Include pictures of Kobra and her family holding hands.

3   Imagine there is war in Australia. Write a diary entry to describe your personal experiences and feelings running away from Australia with your family to go to another safer country by boat.

4   '… like desperate birds who have been let out of their cage.' The writer compared the children running on the streets of Kabul to birds in the above simile. A simile is a figure of speech that is used to describe one thing by comparing it to another. Usually this is done by using words such as 'like', 'seem' or 'as'. Choose one person or a thing from the story and write a simile to describe it.

My Name is Fatima

Research and Discussion

1   When Fatima and her family were escaping their home country Afghanistan to go to Pakistan, policemen stopped them on the border. Although they were travelling illegally, the police let them go because they were bribed. Fatima said talking about this was a taboo even in the family. Why do you think this is the case?

2   By escaping from the Malaysian prison the family in the story put themselves in greater risk of danger. Was the second escape the right decision to make? Did they have an alternative? Why were Fatima and her family willing to risk a second escape attempt? Discuss in groups using examples from the story.

3   What is 'people smuggling'? Why would people trust and give money to the smugglers? What can be done to stop this?

4   How would the children in the story, in particular Fatima's four-year-old brother, be affected by the escape and the unravelling events? Why would Fatima not tell anyone about her ankle?

Writing and Creating

1   Fatima and her family were refugees who had to escape their country because of the violence and the killings. Imagine Fatima and her family did not have war in their country and they wanted to come to Australia. What would they be known as instead of refugees? What are the differences between the two groups? What would be the differences in their journeys? Illustrate this by writing a short travelogue about Fatima's family's legal journey to Australia.

2   Choose a part of the story and change it into a dialogue between the people in that part. For example, the part where a man in Malaysia helped Fatima's dad and his family find a hotel or the part where they escaped from the Malaysian prison.

3   Write the script of the interview that would have taken place between the Australian officers and Fatima's parents at Christmas Island.

The Never-Ending Journey

Research and Discussion

1   The author said he became very afraid when he went to pray in the mosque in Karachi. Find examples of other dangers he faced during his journey to reach Australia. Which ones do you think would be more dangerous for someone of his age and why?

2   The author is from a Hazara background in Afghanistan. When the bus was stopped by the security checkpoint, the policemen came on the bus hitting the other two men who were also from Hazara background. Explain what the author meant by saying 'our only crime was that we were different'.

3   At the start of the story the author describes the journey as a 'gamble with life'. What may be the reasons for a 15-year-old to take a gamble on his life and set out on a journey like this? Did the end justify the means in the story? Explain by giving examples from the story.

Writing and Creating

1   Research and find a map marking the places Syed went to during his journey to Australia. Compare and contrast the country of origin and the destination country using two columns.

2   Reread the story 'The Never-Ending Journey' and draw a timeline of dangers faced and decisions made by Syed during his journey. Choose one of these dangers on the timeline. Describe the emotions Syed would have been going through, using examples from the story.

3   Imagine you got on the same boat with Syed in Indonesia. Retell this part of his journey all the way to Australia in three paragraphs. Include dialogue and use adjectives to describe the people, the places and the time in your retelling.

Same Language, Same Religion
Sayed Hayatullah Mosawi

My family left Afghanistan because of the Taliban. They had killed my uncle – Dad's brother – and my father had been injured in the fight. After that, we left our land … our belongings. I was about six years old.

There were seven of us and we went to Pakistan – my mother, my brother and sister, and two cousins. And, of course, there was my father and I.

During that time, 2003, there was a serious war – violence, fighting, killing and blasting. In Quetta, the city where we lived, they started killing people from the Hazara ethnic background who belong to Shia sect in Islam, as opposed to Sunni sect, like most people in Pakistan. They even killed people praying at the mosque. The killers spoke the same language and were from the same religion as the Taliban.

After my father passed away, my mother started to think about coming to Australia. She borrowed money and I flew alone from Quetta to Malaysia. After that I was put on a boat to Indonesia.

This was going to be the journey of my life. Here is what happened. On the second night, the boat broke down. There was a bad storm. It was raining. The engine stopped. The generator wasn't working and there was no way to get water out of the boat. People were crying and trying to get the water out with buckets. I was shocked. I forgot everything – my mind stopped. Numbness took control of my body, bit by bit. When I tried to shake my foot, I couldn't – it was very heavy.

Eventually, I fell asleep. I dreamed that a man came to me and said, 'No worries'. And he said: 'This is not dangerous for you'. He shook my hand. I tried to kiss his hand as a sign of respect. But when I tried to touch his hand the water came up. The limitless water.

I woke up. I spoke with the other people and said, 'I hope God will help me because the person in my dream said that this was not going to be dangerous for me'.

We made it ashore in one piece. A man came and took us to a jungle.

'Give me 500 dollars per person', he said.

No one had that kind of money so he beat us and threatened to call the police. We lived in the jungle for two or three nights. No water, no food, just dates – 10 dates per person.

Finally, they pushed us all on a bus and drove to Jakarta. We stayed there around two months. Like a prison, we were not allowed to leave the house. Every day I was saying, 'Can you please get us out of here?' However, I did not have any money. Without it, I was not going anywhere. I prayed every day: 'Please God give me money to get out of here'. Every day I called my mother and asked her to get more money. She said, 'Don't worry. I borrowed money'.

When it arrived, I gave it to the agent. Three nights later I was on a leaky boat bound for Australia. I was sick the whole time and lived in fear of being caught by the Indonesian police.

The boat arrived in international waters. I was just beginning to relax a bit when the captain said, 'We are lost'.

The boat drifted for hours. Later that afternoon, a big ship appeared on the horizon. I thought maybe they're Australians coming to rescue us. But others said no, it's the police.

It was the Australian police. They were very nice people, you know. They saved my life. They gave me medicine that soothed the pain. That night I slept soundly on the boat, surrounded by life jackets. I had a good dream but I can't remember what it was.

I lived on Christmas Island for two months. Then I went to Darwin for eight months. After that, immigration sent me to Melbourne. Next I was transferred to Sydney, where the case manager told me that I would have my visa in two weeks.

That was four months ago. I'm still waiting.

All of this time, beginning from Christmas Island till now, I have been in detention. Most of the time I feel … despondent. I am free but not free. I am safe but alone.

When my father passed away, my mother and I took on the responsibility of looking after the children. She and I worked together to take care of the family. I feel lonely here without them.

Postscript: Sayed was granted his permanent visa in January 2012.

Same Language, Same Religion

My Home Country is Afghanistan
Jaweed Rahimi

I loved living with my mother and father. I had three brothers and an uncle. My father had a shop and my uncle was a policeman. Every day after school, I helped my father in the shop and we came home together.

One day my father was distressed. He would not say why. He just said that I could not play in the streets any more and to come to the shop straight after school. At home, he told me to bring him a glass of water. He gathered the family around him and told us that the Taliban had taken my uncle. My father was afraid they had killed him. He finished off by saying that our lives were endangered as well. Soon after, he announced that the family was going to Iran. It was safer there and we could go to school.

Word travelled fast because one afternoon there was a knock at the door. A relative wanted to see my father. I showed her to the living room. She sat down and said, 'I hear you are going'. Father did not deny it so she said, 'How can you leave? Your children were born here. All of the family is buried here. You will be strangers in a strange land. You will be leaving everything you love behind'.

'I don't want to go forever', my father replied. 'I just want to go for five or six years. Then we will come back.' He looked at his three sons and added: 'I want them to be free from fear. Free from all of this. We must go for them … It is dangerous to leave and it is dangerous to stay'.

One of my father's friends had a jeep. He showed up one night and said, 'We leave first thing in the morning'.

We packed some clothes and left our house as soon as it was light. We reached the Pakistan border in the afternoon. That night we stayed in a horrible hotel. It was safe and we had dinner, but I saw huge spiders on the ceiling in the corner and there were big flies everywhere. It was a bit scary.

In the morning we drove to Isfahan, in Iran. My father and my brother found work in a vegetable garden. Life was okay in Isfahan, but one day my brother disappeared. He has not been seen since. My father was so upset he became sick and had to be hospitalised. He was discharged after a week, but he passed away shortly after, leaving his wife alone with two boys.

After that my mother decided to pack up and go to Pakistan. A few years later, my brother came to Australia and he sponsored me to come as well. During my last couple of days in Pakistan I ran around like mad, buying clothes. Then I drove to the airport in Karachi. From there I flew to Bangkok, and from Bangkok to Melbourne.

There were so many different kinds of people there. It was a very exciting time, especially when I started going to language school. After a year, I was transferred to a proper school and started Year 10 classes. I made lots of friends and I've now decided to become a soldier so that I can defend Australia.

My Home Country is Afghanistan

Salt Water
Mohammad Mohsim Jafari

It is with fear that I write the story of my life. I have a superstitious hesitation in lifting the veil on the past because the events I lived through may sound far-fetched and exaggerated. Besides, the task of writing an autobiography is difficult, though a few impressions stand out vividly from the different stages of life. But many of the joys and sorrows of childhood have lost their poignancy; and many incidents of vital importance have been forgotten in the excitement of great discoveries.

In order not to be tedious I shall present only the episodes of my life that are the most interesting and important. Although I am only 17 and haven't experienced much when compared to a 60 or 70-year-old, I have seen more than enough for a teenager.

The first thing you ought to know about me is that I am one of those refugees that came to this country by boat and was kept in a detention centre for a long time.

I was born in 1994, in a town in Helmand province. You might say that I was born during a really bad time in history. My father was killed when I was one. Civil war raged all over Afghanistan, bringing many disasters with it. As if that wasn't bad enough, the Taliban came to power in 1996 and made everything worse. NATO forces came to Afghanistan in 2001 to eliminate them, and war has been raging since.

The other thing you ought to know about me is that I am Hazara, an ethnic minority in Afghanistan that is persecuted by Sunni Muslims. My family and I suffered at their hands. I still remember being beaten badly and stoned on the way to school. When you are little you don't understand why people treat you like this. As I grew older, I realised the same was happening to every Hazara living in the city.

Our school was burned down when I was in Grade 4. My mother was a teacher, so she home-schooled us from there on. But events at the start of 2009 changed my life forever. You see, it was not safe for my mother to be a teacher or even an educated woman. The Taliban and many Pashtuns do not like that; they have strict rules about education and women. Quite simply, they don't go together. And so it was that my mother was taken away from us in that year and I was compelled to leave my homeland.

My only companion was my elder brother. We left everything behind and took refuge in neighbouring Pakistan. We travelled illegally and rented a room in Quetta. I worked in a bakery. After living for a year in Pakistan we realised that it was not a safe place either. The Taliban and al-Qaeda had made inroads here too and they were killing Hazaras on a routine basis. Once again, my brother and I were faced with a dilemma: where to run next?

My brother heard about Australia and, since we did not have enough money for both of us, he decided that I must go alone. He made all the arrangements.

I started the journey with some other guys by going to Malaysia. From there we crossed the border to Indonesia on foot through a forest, walking all day till midnight. Then there was a long car journey to a safehouse. After a week a boat took us to Jakarta. It took three days to get there and the whole time I was scared the police would catch us. But nothing happened and we arrived safe and sound. I hid in a house for almost 25 days.

After that time, I was desperate to just get on a boat and begin the journey to Australia. My wish was granted when, one night, a few local people came and took us to a boat. As you expect, it was small, there was not enough food and far too many people crammed on board – there were 48 of us all together. It was my first time at sea and actually I had never seen an ocean before. It was scary, but it was also good to know that there was a beautiful destination ahead.

It was nearly morning on the first day. Rain was falling. I sat on the edge of the boat, getting drenched. A storm broke and the sea got worse. I honestly thought it was my last day on earth. Huge waves hit the vessel; the sea played it like a toy and tossed us about inside.

Suddenly, a big wave rammed the side of the boat. I slipped and fell into the sea. The water took me under the boat, injuring my right foot

Salt water

very badly. I could not swim and in my panic to stay afloat I thrashed around, swallowing litres of water.

The boat turned around. Someone threw a rope and I managed to haul myself back on board. I was exhausted and my foot was bleeding. I vomited all over the place. Finally, we came to an island. The boat stopped 50 metres from shore and waited for the sea to calm. In the meantime, someone wrapped my foot with a piece of cloth to stop the bleeding.

The journey started again after five or six hours rest. We were at sea for another 12 days until the Australian navy intercepted the boat.

The onboard doctor looked at my foot and said, 'How long have you been in the sea with your foot like that?'

I knew a little bit of English. I said, '12 days'.

He operated on my foot straight away. I got 50 stitches. Three days later we reached Christmas Island. I must have been very hungry and very thirsty because I ate and drank like it was my last meal. Then I slept for almost 30 hours.

There were almost 400 people in the detention facility. All I could see was barbed wire and lots of officers. I was very scared and I thought to myself, 'Why do they want to put me in jail?' I had been told that Australia helped refugees.

This was a very bad time for me. I was on Christmas Island for two months before I was moved to the Darwin detention centre for another nine months. It took almost a year for my application to come through, and then I was given a permanent protection visa.

On 13 April 2011, I got out of detention. Two months after that I came to Melbourne and started school.

One of my teachers asked me, 'How do you feel about coming to Australia?'

I said only one sentence: 'To me it was like coming from darkness to light'.

Same Language, Same Religion

Research and Discussion

1   Find information about detention centres in Australia and Malaysia and do a comparison between the two countries' detention centres. What are they used for? What are the conditions like? When did Australia establish the first detention centre? What are the statistics on how many people are kept in detention centres in both countries? Who are these people? How long has each person been in a detention centre? Finally, write your view on detention centres. Should we keep them or not? Explain your view with information you researched and examples from the story.

2   Find the author's dreams in the story and explain their importance for the story. Explore different layers of meaning in the dreams and try to explain what they meant and how they reflected his state of mind at those moments in time.

3   Although the author is still in detention at the end of the story, what is his view about Australia and the Australian people? Why does he still feel 'despondent'?

Writing and Creating

1   How many times did the author get on a boat to come to Australia? Describe each occasion and the consequences, drawing a table in your books. At the bottom of the table describe his feelings using adjectives such as 'frustrated', 'shocked', 'disappointed' and 'hopeless' in sentences.

2   Work with a partner and find or write song lyrics that best describe the refugees' devastation and hope of finding a safe and happy place to live in the world. Present the song to the class, explaining at the end the meaning and the message of the song.

3   Write a journal entry of the first day the author comes out of the detention centre. Use examples from the story to explain the feelings and the choices of the author about his future life in Australia.

My Home Country is Afghanistan

Research and Discussion

1   Jaweed's father asked him not to waste time after school and go straight to the shop. Why do you think this was?

2   It is a very hard decision for anyone to leave their home country without knowing where to go or what the future holds for them. What were Jaweed's relatives' views on them leaving Afghanistan? Why did Jaweed leave Iran after a few months? Was that a turning point in his life? Explain how this impacted on his life with examples from the story.

3   Why do you think Jaweed decided to be an Australian soldier? What does this show about him and his journey?

4   Jaweed's family drove to Isfahan in Iran from the Afghanistan/Pakistan border. Using the internet, research how far away Isfahan is from this border.

Writing and Creating

1   Write a dialogue that may have taken place between Jaweed and one of his teachers at the language school.

2   Write your own short story entitled 'Leaving My Home Country'. In your story describe your feelings and the difficulties you experienced in the new country, away from Australia, your family and friends.

3   Use a computer to design a glossary of new vocabulary in the story. Share it with others in your class.

Salt Water

Research and Discussion

1   After losing both his parents, the author decided to go to Pakistan with his elder brother. Explain the relationship between the author and his elder brother.

2   The most dangerous part of the author's journey was on a small boat coming to Australia with another 47 people on board. Explain why this was the most dangerous part by giving examples from the story. Why was this the first time the author saw the sea?

3   What is the most dangerous journey you have taken in your life? Was this as dangerous as the one in the story? Discuss with a partner in class.

Writing and Creating

1   Describe the characters, giving examples from the story and using page-long character profiles. Include the author, his elder brother and his father.

2   Write an article for a local newspaper in Australia, covering the story of the author's boat getting intercepted in Australian waters close to Christmas Island.

3   Write a letter to the editor of one of the Australian newspapers, arguing a case for or against having detention centres for refugees and asylum seekers in Australia.

Soccer Ball
Blaise Mupenzi David

I'm 14 years old. I come from a large family – 15 altogether, including five cousins. When I was in Congo, Africa, some of my family members were killed. They took our farms and we decided to leave.

We were very tired when we reached the Kyangwali Refugee Camp in Uganda. A refugee who lived in the camp spoke to my dad in Kiswahili, which is our language. He asked if we were new to the place and my dad said yes. The man told my dad there was nowhere for us to sleep for the night. He said he could take us to the officers in charge. They welcomed us and asked what we were looking for. My father told them that we were looking for somewhere safe and peaceful.

After the officers asked us many questions, they gave us a place where we could grow food and a place where we could build our own house in the camp. Some of the people who spoke Kiswahili helped us build the house out of mud, and grass for the roof. They also taught us how to get along with people in the camp. It took days to build a house. In the meantime, the officers gave us temporary housing. When the house was ready, we moved in and arranged the backyard by cutting the grass that surrounded the place.

My mum made a fire and cooked a meal called *Bugali*, which is made with beans. After dinner, everyone was tired. We wanted to go to bed, but there were no beds. We had to make them ourselves. A group of us went to the forest and cut down trees to make the frames for the mattresses. It was important not to sleep on the ground because of snakes.

My brothers and I went looking for kids to play a game of soccer. But most people had gone to the camp cinemas to watch movies. We had to wait till the next day to find kids who might want to play with us. It was boring in the camp, which is why everyone went to the movies, just to forget where they were for a little while. The cinemas were owned by rich people, who owned farms and had cows, sheep, goats and rabbits.

No one in my family could afford to go to the movies. Soccer was our only entertainment. To be honest, we couldn't even afford to buy a soccer ball and none of the clubs wanted to loan us one.

One day, I came across a team of kids playing soccer. I asked them if I could play and they said yes. After a few games, they made me captain of the team and we started playing against other teams in the village.

On Sunday the family went to church and thanked God for giving us a place to live. After the service I got ready for school the next day. School was compulsory. If you didn't go, security hunted you down and put you in jail for one day! I didn't want to be a prisoner so I went to school. You could only stay home if you were genuinely sick. There were classes Monday to Friday, and sometimes on Saturdays because the teachers wanted students to clean their houses for them. If you didn't show up you got in a lot of trouble.

The headmaster wrote down my name and where I was from. Then he told me to go to Grade 4. In Africa your age doesn't determine your year level; sometimes a 14-year-old can be in Year 4 or Year 3. I was 12 at the time and they put me in Year 4 because I was too smart for Year 3.

All the refugees in Kyangwali grew their own food. People grew many different crops and sold or bartered for things they didn't have. They used the money to buy nice things for their families.

A scary jungle surrounded Kyangwali Refugee Camp. There were snakes large enough to swallow a whole cow. One day, a snake came into our house and my mother had to call my father to come and kill it. From that day onwards, she wanted him to build a safer house.

There were all kinds of dangerous animals living around the camp, but I never saw them. However, others often went hunting in large groups and with dogs. If anything bad happened, they at least had some assistance.

Life is hard in Africa. All the refugees had to walk many kilometres to find clean water. The ones who didn't want to go far, fetched water from dirty swamps. People with bikes filled jerry cans with water and carried them back.

One day two armed men came to our house and demanded to see my father. They wanted to know where the refugee chairman lived. My father told them, but they weren't satisfied. They got very aggressive and started bashing, kicking and pushing our house. They said they were going to kill us because my father deceived them. We were terrified; we didn't sleep at all that night.

They were gone in the morning. My dad went to the refugee camp officers and asked what was going on. He told them exactly what happened. They searched for the men, but they could not find them. After that we were scared to stay there, so they helped us to come to Australia.

I left behind many good friends. Before I went away, I promised them that whatever happens I will never forget them. When you grow up with someone, when you live through good times and bad times together, there's this amazing bond between you. It can never be broken. Leaving those people behind does not feel good.

I like Australia. I am free here. I can do whatever I want, and my parents can afford to send me to school. Thanks to the way they brought me up, I have never been in trouble with the law. That is why I want to thank my parents. And now, I thank the Australian people for letting us into their country.

Jewelled Mirror
Izel Öztürk

The 10th of January 2001 dawned like any other day. Except it wasn't.

It was the day Abra saw her older brother executed. He was only 16 years old. When he refused to join the Taliban, they shot him, point blank, right between the eyes. Abra's brother knew his executioners: they had been childhood friends.

In that moment of horror, as Abra watched her brother drop to his knees, she knew Afghanistan wasn't safe, especially not for a 12-year-old like her. Fear wrapped its fingers around her and gripped like never before. She watched from behind the heavy drapes that separated her sleeping area from that of her brother's. They were beating her mother. Valiantly, she had tried to protect her son. One man spat at her and kicked her aside.

Abra was a beautiful girl. Lean, with long brown hair and big brown eyes, she was intelligent for a girl who had not been to school – not officially anyway. The Taliban had put a stop to that.

When her father came home to find the horror that had been visited upon his family, he wept – for his son and for an uncertain future.

'Our family must survive. It is all we have', he whispered, as they discussed what to do next.

Leaving the country was not going to be easy. Abra's family was used to breaking the law: secretly educating Abra, listening to music and even wearing bright colours and make-up under the burqa. Breaking the law was the only way to take control of their lives.

Abra's father prepared fake passports. Hope and faith filled his thoughts. His prayers were filled with requests for guidance. Fear surfaced but he refused to let it take over. If they were caught, it would not be a jail sentence or a fine, but certain death.

Many long and stressful nights passed before Abra and her family were smuggled over the border into Pakistan.

They travelled at night in the back of an old covered truck. When the truck coughed and spluttered, gasping its last breath, they had to walk. A hole developed on the bottom of Abra's shoe and a blister formed. Soon it became a bloody pulp. Abra had taken a few meagre possessions,

which she carried lovingly under her arm. Her most precious possession was a jewelled hand mirror given to her by her mother. She stared at her reflection, praying that Allah would hold her safely and keep her alive while they undertook this treacherous journey.

Her prayers were answered. From Pakistan they were smuggled into India. This was not a welcoming place. Abra felt as if they were the lowest of the low. They were certainly treated as such. Abra's father cradled her in his arms one desperate night and whispered, 'We may be poor Abra, but we are not poor of heart'.

Abra and her family were taken to a beach with many strangers, mostly Afghanis. Family by family they were hurried onto a very small boat. It was crowded and in each corner there were people who had been through their own horrible journeys. Some wept, some silently stared. Children snivelled and once-strong men quivered. As the days passed, the amount of food and water decreased. It became harder and harder to share.

There was still a long way to go. Thunderclouds danced on the horizon, and then marched towards their tiny, leaky boat. The storm started with one huge almighty bang. It became difficult for the boat to carry on. They had to turn off the engine and remain still, rolling and dipping dangerously through the enormous waves. Abra stared at the darkness of the night, blanketing her world, and wondered if she was ever going to have a normal life, or where she could go to school and not be afraid of getting killed on the way. It was so cold that her fingers and toes were numb. The only thing that warmed her heart was hope. Hope beamed back at her as she stared at the reflection in her tiny jewelled mirror.

In the morning the storm passed. The captain tried the engine, but it wouldn't turn on. Then, towards the back of the boat, an old woman shrieked that water was coming up from beneath her. Panic filled everyone. Almost automatically people began using anything they could find to bail out the water that swirled icily around their feet, while the captain plugged the leak. The water slowed but did not stop completely.

Jewelled Mirror

'You will have to keep using the buckets', he said.

Desperation and fear was in every face. Babies continued to cry, children whimpered, hunger strangled everyone. Abra prayed.

Days passed. People began to lose hope. The old woman became sick and started coughing as if her lungs were about to burst. It was pneumonia. The next morning she was lying motionless on the deck, like a melted clock in Dali's *Persistence of Memory*. She was thrown overboard without ceremony. Her loved ones wept and mourned.

Only a small amount of drinking water remained and there were fights over who deserved it. Abra's mother and father took only a sip and gave the rest to their baby and to Abra.

Abra began to regret leaving Afghanistan. She would've rather died there than be on this boat surrounded by water, dying slowly. She was scared and cried herself to sleep. The warmth that hope had previously given her began to cool off. There was a different face staring back at her from the jewelled mirror. Abra hardly recognised it.

She sat staring into the dim sunrise. Everyone was still asleep. There, in the distance, she saw something that filled her with joy. Was it a trick? No there it was, a ship, close enough to signal. Abra started to wake everyone up. Excitedly, they began yelling and doing the best they could to get the ship's attention, desperate for this chance at survival. They all ran to the side of the boat and began to wave pieces of clothing in the air. Abra's father piled up some rags in a bucket, poured petrol from the engine onto them and threw in a match. Black smoke poured into the sky.

Nothing happened for a while. Then the ship turned and headed towards them. Everyone yelled with joy. There were tears of relief on their faces.

Abra looked into her jewelled mirror and saw a smile. She recognised hope.

When the ship came close, a soldier on board spoke into a megaphone: 'Turn around', he shouted. 'Go back!'

No one understood what he said. But his actions were loud and clear. They were definitely not welcoming.

Abra began to sob. The soldier kept shouting. Others on the boat started to hold their crying babies high in the air. The noise was deafening. The leak in the boat had been forgotten and all of a sudden they realised that the icy water had risen higher; it was up to their knees.

As the ship came closer, the soldiers realised that the boat was in trouble and its human cargo perilously close to death. Abra watched from behind her father as four soldiers climbed into a small rubber boat and headed in their direction, guns pointed squarely at them.

'When will this nightmare end?' Abra asked herself, as the four soldiers clambered into the leaky vessel. She was terrified. She thought they were going to kill her. There had been talk of pirates, but surely they could not pose as soldiers. The soldiers spoke quickly and aggressively to the captain. He was handcuffed and taken away. As the soldiers approached the huddled group, they lowered their guns and the one who seemed to be in charge spoke softly – in Afghani. Abra's heart skipped a beat.

It took hours to get all of the people off the sinking boat.

Abra stared into her jewelled mirror. Only this time she couldn't see her reflection for the tears streaming from her eyes.

The trip to Darwin was uneventful. Abra was not hungry, thirsty or in immediate danger. But she was not at peace. Sleep did not come and she was nervous.

They arrived in Darwin late in the afternoon. They were separated and interviewed. How much money did you pay to get here? Who brought you? Why did you leave? Do you have family back in Afghanistan?

The questions were endless. Abra was questioned with her family and then alone. She wondered why she needed to be interviewed at all. It seemed obvious to her. She just wanted to be safe and alive. She became upset at the thought of them not accepting her family into Australia. If they didn't, would they send them back? They couldn't go back, and they most certainly didn't want to.

When the interviews were over, Abra sat silently with her family. While clutching her jewelled mirror, she thought of her dead brother.

The words 'a safe place' swam around her head.

Jewelled Mirror

'What is a safe place?' Abra asked her father.

'It is where the government is going to put us while they decide our fate, my jewel', he responded quietly. 'There is a place in the outback of South Australia called Woomera. It is called a detention centre.'

Abra boarded the small plane first, excited by the prospect of flight. Her mother and father, however, were not. This didn't feel right. They were on the plane for hours. It was dark when they landed. It was impossible to see. A large bus pulled up near the plane and they were herded on to it, like human cattle, shoving and pushing their way forward. The darkness of the Australian outback enveloped them. The bus sped away. When it stopped they were in front of a building that looked like a box. They were given a little room, with strange beds on top of each other. Abra placed her mirror on top of her pillow. She didn't dare to look into it.

In the morning she woke up and looked out the window. It was terrifying. They were in the middle of a desert. In her family's little room were two old dirty bunk beds. Upon the window were torn and dusty curtains. There were too many people and not enough rooms. There was a tall metal fence around the detention centre, as tall as two large men. On top of this fence was wire as sharp as razors. Inside the fence was another fence.

Abra couldn't believe her eyes. It was a prison. The worst sort of prison you could imagine because its prisoners all dreamed of one thing: freedom.

Abra was given a number. Her mother was given a similar number, as was her father. Abra saw that everyone inside the detention centre got one. It represented who they were. Abra asked one of the soldiers where they were. 'Hell', he said.

Hell it might have been, but it was boring. There was nothing to do. Abra was made to attend a makeshift school. But it was clear that the teacher did not care for her or any of the children. All day people sat around; sickness was everywhere. Boredom took over. The children kicked a soccer ball. Abra hated ball games. Even the food was freakishly disgusting. Abra appreciated that at least she was not hungry. Still, she longed for a traditional meal prepared lovingly by her mother. In the morning they were given cornflakes with milk; their lunch was a sandwich, often made with stale bread and soggy lettuce, something she had never eaten before and wished to never eat again. Dinner was always rice with chicken. Abra thought that would taste fine, if they could only cook the rice and chicken properly.

Interview after interview was conducted. Abra always brought her jewelled mirror and sat quietly staring into it, willing the outcome to be favourable. She watched her face wrinkle as each tear fell silently down her cheek. Tuesday and Thursday were called 'visa days', when people found out if they were allowed to leave this place. Abra listened carefully to the soldiers on visa days to see if her family's name was called. It never was. Abra's mother pleaded with the soldiers to let them leave. People left every week, but it seemed that it would never be their turn. There was talk of rioting. But Abra's father was adamant: violence will never help you.

Abra celebrated two birthdays in detention. At 14 she was still a beautiful girl but her big brown eyes had dulled. Her family was used to living in a prison. Crying was of no use. Every week or so they watched as new people arrived in this tragic place. They entered with a smile on their faces and ended up with a heartbreaking frown. There was very little laughter, even from children.

Abra didn't talk to anyone. She became a lifeless statue. She didn't find the need to talk because everyone's stories were the same. Some days she gazed at her reflection in the mirror and thought about all the other young women around the world. They were free. They had a better life.

Visa days continued to come and go. One morning, as the soldiers called out the numbers, Abra sat up with a start.

'Numbers 1473, 1478, 1398, 375 and 396, please come to the administration complex. I repeat, numbers 375 and 396.'

Abra's heart skipped a beat before she realised they were calling her family's numbers. She couldn't believe her ears. Her father disappeared for what seemed like hours. In reality it was only a matter of minutes. He returned to announce that they must gather their belongings and board the bus.

As Abra entered the bus, she kept pinching herself to make sure it wasn't a dream. In one hand she had a plastic bag with her few possessions and in her other her precious mirror. She held it before her and watched as her face lit up, this time with tears of joy. She took one last look at the place that had been home for the past two years and wished it all away. Blew it from her mind's eye.

Abra and her family were taken to Adelaide and awarded refugee status. Abra knew deep inside that life was still an uncertain journey of ups and downs, but she truly believed that this was the beginning. The violent death of her older brother and the oppression suffered by her family had set them on an incredible journey.

After what she had experienced, she felt sorry for the people who were still at the detention centre, and this was her motivation. Abra dreamed of becoming a lawyer and of making a change in her world – to help and protect those in need.

Abra will be the jewelled reflection for a just society.

Home
Zahra Ali

War engulfed Afghanistan in the late 1970s when Russia tried to expand its borders. Many people left the country at that time, seeking safety as Russia and America fought over Afghanistan. When the Russians left, Afghanistan was in turmoil. They left behind a legacy of landmines and unexploded artillery. Political unrest followed and the Taliban came to power. Many Afghanis lost their homes, families were separated and people died. Others lost limbs by stepping on landmines. Afghanis killed Afghanis. Hazaras killed Kandari people. The ones who wanted no part of this conflict simply left.

Abbas was one of them. At 21, he had many responsibilities. His mother depended on him. His wife, Zeniab, and the two children, Amir and Fatima, were Abbas's world. Still, he had to make a better future for his wife and children. It was a risk, but he had no choice. He left without knowing if he would ever see them again.

It was a freezing January night in 2000. Four friends joined Abbas on the journey. Together they travelled to Pakistan and after three months made their way to Indonesia. Australia was their ultimate goal. They spent what little money they had on buying passage on a boat. The people smuggler was hardly trustworthy, but again Abbas and his friends had no choice. They had to trust him or remain in limbo.

Abbas was on the boat for 14 days, with barely a drink of water. The daily meal was rice. What kept him going was the vision of his beloved family, his precious wife and their children, while he prayed. When he had almost given up hope, the Australian navy appeared on the horizon.

The reception was not what Abbas had expected. He was ordered to go back to where he came from. Shame filled him as he tried to explain how desperate he was. Almost defeated and wishing death upon himself, Abbas looked up to one of the sailors who appeared to be reasonable. The sailor extended his hand to help Abbas to his feet.

'Come on, mate', he said. 'You must get off this leaky boat.'

What shocked Abbas was that the man was speaking in a language he understood. Sailors in their pressed uniforms and clean shoes eyed them

Home

suspiciously. The kind sailor provided a buffer between the refugees and the other men. Officers then began their investigations. Language was their barrier and frustration began and ended every interview.

After two days, Abbas and the other boat people were transferred to Darwin. Almost immediately, Abbas found himself on an aeroplane to Woomera. This was the detention camp he had heard about. Fear gripped him. He had no idea what awaited him and no way to contact his wife.

While Abbas braved his journey, his beautiful wife, his children and his mother began their own journey to freedom. The family moved to Pakistan where they lived with another Hazara family. Abbas, of course, did not know this. In Woomera Detention Centre he lived in a small room with four people. In the beginning he didn't have any contact with the outside world. It was like a jail; he missed his family and worried deeply for their safety.

He was interviewed every week and asked about his family and where he had came from. At every interview he was asked different questions, just to make sure that he was not lying and then he was moved to a different room.

In one of these rooms, Abbas was amazed to discover an old but working television. He searched for news from his homeland, news of the world. There was nothing. It was as if he and the other refugees did not exist.

'How could this be?' he wondered. 'People must understand how it is for us.'

News leaked out about the goings-on at Woomera. People in the outside world found out that it was overcrowded and had poor sanitation. Before long, reporters were given access to the centre. Abbas saw his opportunity and seized it. A woman from The Associated Press interviewed various people. Abbas made sure he was one of them. She published Abbas's story in a leading newspaper. At the time Abbas could not know how important that would be in finding his family.

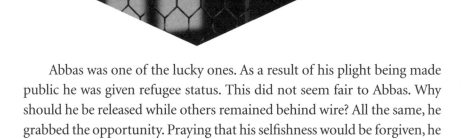

Abbas was one of the lucky ones. As a result of his plight being made public he was given refugee status. This did not seem fair to Abbas. Why should he be released while others remained behind wire? All the same, he grabbed the opportunity. Praying that his selfishness would be forgiven, he set forth to create a new life in Australia and to find his family.

When Abbas left the camp he lived with an old couple in Victoria. He picked grapes in a vineyard. The couple helped him with his English, found a place for him to live and kept him employed. Just as Abbas settled into his new life his prayers were answered.

He received a letter from *The Australian* newspaper.

What it said sent shivers up Abbas's spine. His family had been found. They were safe and living in Pakistan. After they escaped, they lived in a refugee camp. Little did Abbas know but the reporter who he had spoken to at the Woomera Detention Centre had travelled to his war-torn country. She had visited the camps in Pakistan. Word of her investigations led her to Abbas's wife, and for Abbas a happy ending.

Abbas worked hard to reunite his family. He lived in Melbourne for a few years and then moved to Adelaide. He saved meticulously, accounting for his every cent. In time, he became an Australian citizen. His aim was to return to Pakistan and bring his family to Australia. A few years later he flew to Pakistan and found his beloved wife, children and his mother. When Abbas escaped his oppressed country, his son Amir was barely six months old. He was now 10. His daughter Fatima was on the cusp of womanhood. It was a very touching reunion.

But a further struggle awaited Abbas. He was not permitted to bring his mother to Australia, only his wife and children. How could he leave her behind? His mother gently cradled his face and he knew that she was giving him permission to leave, despite her heartbreak. Abbas boarded a plane with his wife and children and flew away.

The family bought a house in Adelaide. After a while they adjusted to the new language and culture. It was hard; people were often mean

Home

and did not understand. Abbas worked hard as a bus driver. His children started school and Zeniab opened a beauty salon exclusively for Muslim women. The business thrived.

One night, Abbas questioned himself. 'Everything is going great for me', he said, 'but the feeling of sadness about leaving my country and my real home still remains'.

Deep down he wanted to go back so that his children could learn about their country. Is the loss of his culture the price he must pay for a safer future for himself and his children?

He will never forget the things that he has been through. Afghanistan is his home, where he was born and grew up. He hopes that his country will go back to the way it was, when he was young. People were free to go about and children could play outside without fear. Abbas quietly talked about these things with his wife. He said, 'I hope that one day the government in Afghanistan will make it safe for people to return. So that people won't have to leave their motherland; won't have to go far from home'.

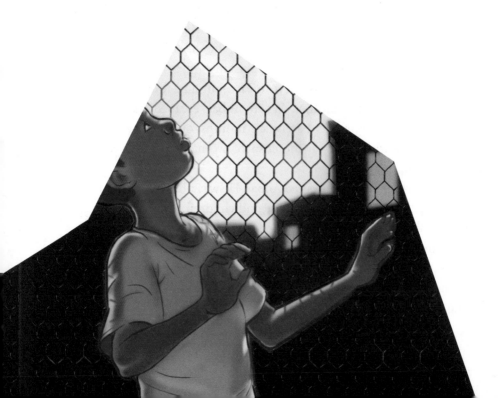

Soccer Ball

Research and Discussion

1   Blaise left behind his home and all his friends when he escaped the conflict in Congo. Although at first he did not have friends at the refugee camp, he made many friends playing soccer. Do you remember when you first made friends at school? Tell the person next to you how you made new friends in Year 7 when you first came to the school. What is your view on sports bringing people together?

2   Blaise and other children had to go to school five, sometimes six, days a week at the camp. If they failed to go to school one day, the children were put in jail. The situation is very different in Australia. Why do you think the punishment for missing school is so harsh at Kyangwali Refugee Camp? List some of the other differences between life in Kyangwali Refugee Camp in Uganda and life in Australia.

3   The refugee camps at Kyangwali and in other parts of Africa show the extent of poverty and disease in that country, compared to other countries in the world. If you had the power to change something for the better in Africa, what would you do?

4   Rewrite this story reversing the journey to Africa from Australia and characters into Australians instead of Africans.

Writing and Creating

1   Instructional writing is a kind of writing that includes advice and direction on *how* something is done. Some examples of common instructional texts include recipes and manuals. The story 'Soccer Ball' is written in the first person voice. Change the voice to the second person and use the information in the story to write an instructional piece titled 'How to Live Happily in Kyangwali Refugee Camp'. Include instructions and advice about housing, schools, food, dangers and people in your writing.

2   Write a personal letter from Blaise to his soccer teammates at Kyangwali Refugee Camp, telling them about the changes in your life in Australia.

3   Draw or make a 3D model of the Kyangwali Refugee Camp based on the information in the story.

Jewelled Mirror

Research and Discussion

1   Abra and her family went through tough times before, during and after their journey to Australia. Discuss the stages of their journey in class. Describe the difficulties experienced by Abra and her family that are different to the experiences of children and families in Australia.

2   Who were the soldiers who saved Abra and everyone on the leaky boat? Where did they take everyone? Find information about the town Woomera and describe it.

3   Based on Abra's descriptions, what kind of place is Woomera Detention Centre? Describe using examples from the story.

4   Prepare a class debate on the topic 'Should Australia ban mandatory detention centres?' Organise groups of for and against in class to argue a case in the debate. Use examples from the story to support your arguments.

Writing and Creating

1   The story's title is used as a special symbol by the author. We are almost led to see the story through the reflections in the mirror, which becomes as one with Abra by the end of the story. Explain in a paragraph the importance of the jewelled mirror and what it represents by providing examples.

2   The author uses many examples of figurative language and imagery. In doing so, she uses language tools such as metaphor, simile and personification. Find the definition for each of these. Draw a table with two columns and write the examples below in the first column. In the second column write which of the language tools are being used in the examples. Finally, find other examples of figurative language techniques in the story and add them to your table.

    a   'Thunderclouds danced on the horizon, and then marched towards their tiny, leaky boat.'

    b   'Hope beamed back at her as she stared at the reflection in her tiny jewelled mirror.'

    c   '… hunger strangled everyone.'

    d   '… like a melted clock in Dali's *Persistence of Memory*.'

    e   '… human cargo …'

    f   'The words "a safe place" swam around her head.'

    g   'The darkness of the Australian outback enveloped them.'

3   Explain briefly what Izel Öztürk meant by the following sentences.

    a   'Abra will be the jewelled reflection for a just society.'

    b   'Breaking the law was the only way to take control of their lives.'

    c   'We may be poor, Abra, but we are not poor of heart.'

    d   'The worst sort of prison you could imagine because its prisoners all dreamed of one thing: freedom.'

Home

Research and Discussion

1   Each year, many countries in the world offer their help to refugees. Some help more than others. Do you think rich countries should be forced to help refugees more? Does Australia accept and help refugees the way it should, compared to other wealthy countries? Find statistics on world refugee intake and discuss this issue in class.

2   The first time Abbas met the Australian Navy, some soldiers bullied him and told him to go back to where he came from. How do you think this made Abbas feel after he had been on a boat for 14 days? What is your view of the treatment of refugees in Australia?

3   Zahra Ali's story explores the concept of 'home'. She believes that people who leave their home and move to another country will never live their culture and traditions as they would have in their home country. Hence, they will never fully belong to the new place they moved to. Do you agree with her? Explain your answer with examples.

Writing and Creating

1   In pairs or small groups, prepare and present a three-minute oral presentation about the issue of world refugees.

2   Find two people who are from a refugee or a migrant background and interview them about their journey to Australia. Report your findings to the class.

3   Based on the story, do you think detention centres are an ideal place for refugees? Are there detention centres in other wealthy countries? Are there more effective and quicker alternatives to detention centres? Devise a strategy to improve detention centres for refugees coming to Australia. Illustrate or describe your strategy in detail.

Counter 27
Azaara Perakath

'Now what?' she muttered. Finding a different nursery rhyme or fairytale to read to her daughter before bed each night was challenging at times. There didn't seem to be any stories left on the shelf that the little girl hadn't heard.

The hallway was dimly lit. An old wooden bookcase stood in the corner. In front of it the silhouette of a young woman stood atop a ladder, wringing her hands in despair. Her lustrous curls cascaded around her face as she strained her eyes, willing a book to materialise out of thin air. Then, between two paperback illustrated stories, she caught sight of a brown hardcover with faded gold lettering on the spine. Curious, she reached for it but couldn't get her hand far enough into the narrow gap. She continued to struggle, watching in frustration as her fingertips brushed against the leathery spine. She paused to wipe her clammy palms on her jeans and then, with a heavy sigh, extended her arm and grabbed the leather between her fingers, carefully bringing it down from the shelf.

She propped the ladder up against the wall and walked into her daughter's room. Sitting on the edge of the bed, she opened the book, carefully unfolded the dog-eared pages, and blew the dust away from where it had settled in the binding. She stayed motionless for a few seconds, admiring the faded lines of the paper and enjoying the crisp sound as she turned each page.

Wide-eyed and inquisitive, the child sat under the covers. 'Go on Mum! Which bedtime story will it be tonight?'

The woman smiled, touched by the little girl's enthusiasm. 'Well, this story is one you would not have heard before. It's a tale of self-belief and breaking boundaries.' In a melodious voice, she began to read:

'Sunlight glinted off the glass terminal of Hong Kong International Airport. Outside taxis waited, forming a red army amidst the hoards of people milling near the entrance. Each time the sliding doors parted, a buzz of expectancy engulfed the airport, as people prepared to embark on the first stage of their journeys across the globe.

'And that's exactly what it was for the girl waiting at counter number 27. Standing with her suitcase in tow, she realised how small and insignificant we are as individuals in the grand scheme of things. She watched various scenes play out before her, like a pantomime without pre-defined stage directions.

'Luggage was loaded onto the platform at the check-in desk, coupled with the reassuring smiles of staff as boarding passes were issued. Meanwhile, the air-conditioning system whirred, a great monster humming in its sleep. Groups of people were scattered at random, dreaming of their destinations, while children ran about, constantly on the move, to expend their boundless energy.

'She turned to her younger sister and smiled. The girl nodded in acknowledgement, sharing her excitement. Though an outsider would never guess the story of their lives, the sisters had endured many hardships and compromises. They knew that migrating to Australia offered their family the prospect of hope and new beginnings.

'She remembered the countless hours they had spent packing their possessions, as though trying to preserve little pieces of their old lives to combine with the new and unfamiliar. Closing her eyes, she paused to appreciate everything that Hong Kong had offered her.

'By day, it was a bustling metropolis; by night, a city illuminated by the lights and the vibrancy of the people. The street hawkers, the old-style trams, the nauseating but strangely comforting smells of dried seafood and other traditional delicacies. These were all things that characterised Hong Kong as a unique place, a melting pot for a multitude of cultures, and a place she had grown to love. And yet, inside, she felt a sense of relief – a change would do them all good.

'In the Southern Hemisphere, things would be different. Christmas would no longer be a winter festival, there would be an ease of communication, road trips would include sightings of Australia's many indigenous animals, and the lifestyle will be relaxed, free from the obligations that come with traditional life. This was what their family needed, to sever the ties that bound them to their old life and start anew, in an entirely different continent, as foreigners, with a renewed perspective.

'Looking up at the great arches of the airport ceiling with its skylight design, she watched as the late afternoon sun made way for dusk. The sky was painted a vivid shade of crimson, set ablaze with brilliant streaks of red and orange. It was as if a sari had been draped across it, reminding her of her Indian roots.

'She sometimes wished that she had been exposed to more of her heritage. Being unable to speak even one of the many Indian dialects and having lived outside India all her life, she felt like an outsider looking in. Yet she still recalled the many childhood experiences that she had had when visiting her grandparents in Bangalore. The incessant beeping of horns during rush hour created a discordant racket while men wheeled carts through the streets, stocked with colourful fruits and other wares. The familiar smells that permeated the air, of freshly ground spices and the sweet fragrances of sandalwood or almond oil and jasmine flowers.

'India had always been a country steeped in customs and traditions. Being Indian had opened her eyes to how fortunate she was to have access to little luxuries, which are often taken for granted in the developed world and mean so much to those living in poverty. She began to wonder whether she would be accepted in Australia, despite her international background. She had always felt completely at ease in Hong Kong. But what if she could no longer enjoy the things she had grown accustomed to?

'With these thoughts foremost in her mind, the family moved through immigration and security screening. The wait seemed never-ending. Each time she stole a glance at the clock on her phone, time seemed to stand still, gently mocking her. Finally, they boarded the flight, and it seemed to her that she was stepping into a portal to a new world.

'A dirt road led to the house, which was off the beaten track in the rural town of Murray Bridge. During the drive, they marvelled at the change in landscape. Where there had been skyscrapers and densely populated concrete communities, there were now small, flat buildings and vast open spaces. This was so different from what she had expected.

'People, old and young, were out and about, some running errands, others enjoying a leisurely stroll. These signs of activity cheered her up considerably. She was beginning to see the advantages of living in a place like Australia. She had envisioned Adelaide to be a small and nondescript city, a place with a dearth of life compared to Hong Kong. Yet in the mere minutes after her arrival on Australian soil, her eyes had been opened to the broader picture.

'As she watched the world speed by from the car window, she saw cows grazing in fields, unperturbed by the traffic. Fields of canola lined the freeway, many flecks of yellow on a blank canvas. The traffic flowed freely with every dip and curve in the Adelaide Hills.

'A wave of fatigue overcame her. Leaning her head against the car window, she drifted off into another realm.

'Waking up in the new house, she saw ground frost beyond her window, finely woven between soil and grass, like a spider's silken web, each intricate glassy shard a reminder of the harsh reality of trying to belong in a cold and unforgiving world. She knew that various family members would send judgements along the telephone wires from across the globe, from India to America, attempting to discourage the family from taking this step, planting the seeds of doubt in their minds.

"Australia is too far away from family."

"What about your roots?"

"How will you manage in a strange place with no one to help you?"

'All were comments that hindered the process of settling in. And yet there existed a strange sense of fearlessness. As though embracing their individuality would only shape and mould them into educated, more balanced people. Yet there were still many challenges to face. Including that dreaded day: the first day of school.

'As she walked through the school gates, she envisioned herself as a famed actress playing the role of the "new girl". It was a label she would have to overcome to earn the respect of her peers. She heard them, in the corridors, by the lockers, lingering outside classrooms. Glances were thrown in her direction, followed by whispered conversations. It was not as if she had not dealt with any of this before. But with age, it becomes harder to acknowledge the challenges of starting over.

'She felt disoriented, but soon realised that the faces were friendly and welcoming, accepting her as a member of their established community. It became easier as she fought to find a place for herself and she began to find the light in the darkness.

'In early October it was time to set the clocks forward to comply with the daylight saving scheme. As she wound the hands of her alarm clock, she saw her journey flash before her.

'Defying the distances posed by oceans and rivers, and voyaging across land and sky, beginning a new life abroad had been just one step in the process of seeking redemption. One family's choices and everything that followed happened by chance. But that is how they found themselves on the path to true happiness.'

The woman closed the book.

'Mum, that was a great story!' the little girl said. 'I could see all those places, and I felt as if I knew that girl. It was much better than those old stories you tell me. Who is the little girl? Who is the author?'

'Well, darling,' her mother replied, tears welling up in her eyes, 'that girl … was me'.

Roshan's Voice
Roshan Jafari

I was born in a village called Haidar Jaghori. I don't have much information about Afghanistan because I was little when my family moved to Pakistan. All I know is that life was not easy.

It was especially hard for girls. It was forbidden for them to be educated. They could not go out alone and they could not marry the man they wanted. Their parents gave them to whoever made a marriage proposal, no matter how old they were. I am not saying this was the parents' fault; they didn't know any better and they did what they thought was best for their daughters.

Everything was new for me in Pakistan, especially speaking Urdu. It takes time to learn a language properly and it was not easy for me. But I had no choice. I had to make the best out of every situation. Let's face it, every country is different and no place can be the same as your own lovely soil.

After some years in Pakistan, my brother sponsored us to go to Australia. It took about two years to be accepted.

My first wish was to learn English. I wanted to communicate with the ease and confidence of a cousin who had come here before us. It was amazing to listen to her talk. I used to say, 'I wish I was like you' and she said, 'Do not worry. You can do it too very soon'.

The first thing I did was to enrol in English classes through a migrant settlement program. I started off by reading simple books. By the second week I was able to ask for directions and to do simple things by myself. I guess you can say that I was confident; I was definitely not shy or embarrassed about making a fool of myself when my language capabilities did not match my thoughts.

My English is still not as good as it can be. But I think we all have to be patient when achieving a goal. Life is definitely not easy. I think we all have to face the good and the bad in life. I am glad to be in Australia. My aim is to get a proper education and help people, especially girls. One day I would like to write a book about all of this and share my experiences with other people who, for whatever reason, are struggling.

Someone to Call a Friend
Kpana Bolay

I came to Findon High School
I knew no one, not even the teachers
I was so shy
I always stood by myself
Everything around me was creepy
Students walked past me so fast
Like a bullet passing through someone
The school was old
The sunlight was shining through my eyes
It is a new day for me
I walked up to some of the popular girls
Who were standing close to the school oval
I said 'Hello my name is Sarafina'
They looked me up and down and giggled
'What a stupid name', they said
I heard what they said but I chose to ignore them
I couldn't face the embarrassment
I cried and walked past them
First day at school
The bell rang
Time for me to go to class
Time for me to meet my new classmates
Time for me to meet my new teacher
On my way to home classroom
My eyes clapped on this handsome boy
I was out of breath for a minute
Since I came on campus, no one
Spoke to me but he did
He helped me out
I told him thank you!
Time for class

When I came to Findon High School
I knew no one
No one understood the way I felt
I was on the edge
Trying to get through life
I felt like I was in a cave
In front of the school
Frozen in my steps
Standing
The breeze flicked my hair back and forth
I struggled to get into class
To meet my teacher
She was there when I was sad
She asked me if I'm okay
I said I will be fine
Tears fell down my cheek
She always knew that I was really not okay
You have touched my life in so many ways
You showed me right from wrong
You stood close to me like a friend
And this is what makes you
Not just any kind of teacher
But a soul mate
I trust my teacher
I trust her more than
My mum and dad
My friend
I trust her with my life
I feel like I can tell her
How I feel about everything
And she will understand
She is always there for me
Supporting me

And listening to me
When I need to talk to her
You are like a god sent from heaven
Teachers are more than
Someone you can call a friend.

Someone to Call a Friend

Counter 27

Research and Discussion

1   Who was the girl standing at counter 27 and where was she travelling? Describe her, giving examples from the story.

2   What did the rest of the family members think about her family's decision to migrate? Find the reasons in the story why family members thought they should not have left and then list the reasons why you think the family made the right decision. Give examples from the story to support your reasons.

3   The author believes that 'with age, it becomes harder to acknowledge the challenges of starting over'. Do you agree?

4   Explain what the author meant by 'just one step in the process of seeking redemption'. What kind of redemption do you think the author is talking about? Think of examples of redemption possible for her and her family.

Writing and Creating

1   Read the author's description of Hong Kong and Australia. Choose another country and describe it in the same way. In your description include a sentence or a phrase for each of the five senses: hearing, seeing, tasting, touching and smelling.

2   The writer used strong imagery and figurative language for clear description: '… the air-conditioning system whirred, a great monster humming in its sleep'. What kind of figurative language tool is used in the above quotation? Find other examples of figurative language use: words and phrases the author used for descriptions of places and people.

3   Imagine you are Azaara. Write a short piece explaining what it's like to be a second generation immigrant living in Australia. Does Australia feel like home to you? Are you interested in finding out more about your heritage and family history?

Roshan's Voice

Research and Discussion

1   The writer talks about the difficulties of being a girl in Afghanistan. What sort of difficulties and inequalities do Afghani girls face, according to the story? How can this be changed?
2   How did Roshan's life change in Australia? How did she manage to improve her English in such a short period of time?
3   The story 'Roshan's Voice' has a lot to say about adapting, change and the influence of a new place on our lives. Find examples for each one. What is the author's main message about change in the story?

Writing and Creating

1   Work with the person next to you and write the script for Roshan's speech on 'Young Afghani Refugees in Australia' to be delivered during the school assembly.
2   Using the information in Roshan's story about how she managed change in her life in Australia, write a guide for new refugee students starting at your school. Include all the support available for them at your school.
3   Roshan wants to write a book about her experiences as a refugee and the hardships she has overcome. Write the blurb for Roshan's book using Roshan's story as inspiration.

Someone to Call a Friend

Research and Discussion

1   How did Kpana feel on the first day of school in Australia? What happened that made her feel this way? Discuss.

2   Why did Kpana feel like she was 'in a cave' or 'on the edge' on the way to the class? Do you think she had problems before coming to school? Find out how many students there are like Kpana at your school who are new to Australia and to your school. Explain why, like Kpana, they may be feeling lost and helpless at the school.

3   How did Kpana describe her teacher? Why? Give examples from the poem.

4   Think of your first day at school and how you felt. What are the similarities and the differences? Explain these by giving examples from the poem.

Writing and Creating

1   Kpana's poem starts off in the first person. Towards the end it changes to second person and then back to first person. Discuss and write with a partner the reasons for Kpana's switching to second person just for that part.

2   Kpana makes use of similes to describe some of the people and the places in her poem. Find each example of simile in the poem and explain its meaning.

3   Make a list of actions you, your friends, teachers and the principal can take to make students like Kpana feel welcome and at ease.

A New Beginning
Maisam Haidari

I was born in a small village called Zerack. I have three brothers and one sister. My mother and father married in Afghanistan and my father came to Australia soon after I was born.

I started going to school with my big brother Rohollah when I was seven years old. It was much better than sitting at home and doing nothing except helping my mother. Each day when my brother came home from school I ran to him and helped him carry his school bag. When I started going to school with him I found out just how tired he must have been. There was no public transport and we had to walk many miles to school.

Each day I got up at six o'clock in the morning. First I had to pray with my mother and brother. Then we ate breakfast and rushed off. Classes were from 9 a.m. to 12 p.m., six days a week. For lunch, students brought bread and a bottle of water, or something else to drink. After school we played outside with friends. Electricity was expensive and we couldn't afford things like television.

My father came to Australia to find a good job and send the money home to support his family. There wasn't much to eat or drink in Zareck. People were very poor. The money my father sent helped pay for a lot of things we needed, like electricity and water.

The main reason my family left Afghanistan was because of the Taliban. Americans had been fighting the Taliban for years but there was no end to the war. My father wrote and told my mother to move to Kabul. The family lived in Kabul for a few months and then moved to Pakistan. My father was sponsoring us to come to Australia. All together it took about two years to organise everything. During that time, my brother and I went to English school so that we would speak the language better when we came here.

Some students at the school were also trying to migrate to Australia. I asked my mother why are we going to Australia. She replied, 'We will be much safer and have our own freedom, our own rights'. She sounded happy.

There was me thinking that my family was going to Australia for a holiday.

A New Beginning

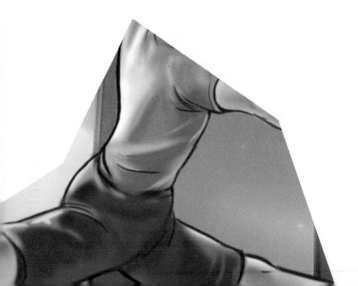

Then, one very happy day, my father called to say we could go and live with him in Australia. We packed our stuff and a week later we headed for the airport. I felt sad because I knew I would miss my country. But it was also exciting that my family was going to be together. My sister and brothers were also happy and sad for pretty much the same reasons. We would all miss Afghanistan, but we were happy to be going someplace safe.

Life here is very different. We now have all the things we couldn't afford in Afghanistan, and our parents drop us off at school in a car.

The Unexpected Child
Robert Matyus

I was an unexpected child. My mum didn't want me. God appeared in her dreams and told her not to get rid of me. You will regret it, He told her. If he lives, your little boy will be handsome, famous and rich. My mum changed her mind. When I arrived, the nurse told her that I was very handsome and that I will be a ladies man.

While growing up in Romania, I would dream of what it would be like to have everything you want. You are famous, happy, successful, and have your own family.

In reality I never had any of these things. I was the skinny boy who didn't know the popular kids in the school. After my mum broke up with my dad when I was two years old, we lived by ourselves. There was my mum, my older sister and me. Mum worked and there were times when we didn't have anything to eat.

I had a happy childhood and, despite everything, I've had a blessed life. I spent most of my time having fun with my friends, playing soccer and running around like mad. I never studied, but somehow I always passed with good marks. Mum used to say that I have a good memory and that I can remember everything that happens in class. Maybe she's right. In Year 7 people asked me what I want to do and I always said, 'I don't know'.

There was this dance show on TV. It was called *America's Best Dance Crew*. I used to watch it no matter what. It didn't matter if I had other stuff to do, this was the most important thing during the week. Maximum volume.

It probably drove my neighbours crazy. I didn't care. Seeing people dance made me happy! I used to jump around the house when they did those crazy moves, like head spin. I wanted to be like them, but I didn't know where to start.

At that time, my mum was going out with a very nice guy. It turns out that he was her first boyfriend from when she was 16. They went out for two years and then broke up. The next time they saw each other was when she'd gone to the police station to get a new ID and he was there

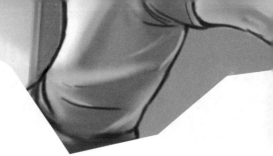

getting a new passport. They hadn't seen each other for 27 years. They started talking and realised they still liked each other. Mum told me he lives in Australia. I was a bit surprised because I'd never met anybody who lived in that country.

To cut a long story short, they married and we moved to Australia. The trip took about 24 hours. The view was amazing from up high. At the airport, I had to do all the work because my mum didn't speak English. My stepdad picked us up and drove to a restaurant close to our home. The sky was clear and the stars were bright. I realised that maybe Australia might not be so bad after all.

A few weeks later, my stepfather enrolled me in an English language school. I was a bit shy on the first day, but people were friendly and they showed me around. I made friends with everybody. A couple of days later we had to choose our electives. There was basketball, soccer, cricket, IT and many more.

One elective captured my attention: dancing.

When I heard the word 'dancing' my heart started beating really fast. I got really excited.

My first thought was that I'm not a good dancer, but I love watching it and maybe this is my chance to give it a try. So I did.

At the beginning, I was one of the worst dancers in the class. But it did not matter to me because I loved what I was doing. My love for dancing grew each day. I started practising and wanting to improve as much as possible. A few weeks later, during an English class, a young woman came in and gave everybody a piece of paper. The following week there was going to be a dance audition for a scholarship. I couldn't believe my eyes.

'No matter what,' I said to myself, 'I'm going to have that scholarship. I'm going to practise and win'.

I practised every day for up to five hours. The big day came. I was excited and ready. There were 20 dancers at the audition. That gave me second thoughts, but then I told myself, 'I can do this' and focused on that.

There were three stages to the audition: a piece of choreography for the whole class, a freestyle solo session and a written exercise where you answer questions like, 'What does dance make you feel like?' and 'What would you do if you won?'

I left that day knowing I did a good job.

Later that week, I was told that I won the scholarship. I did not know how to react. My hands were shaking, my heart was beating fast and I couldn't speak. I hugged everybody and said my thank yous. I was so happy.

Miss Claire, my dance teacher at Noble Park, taught me that as a dancer, your body is the pencil and the dance floor is the canvas, and you are making art through your movements. I started going to professional hip-hop studios, meeting professional dancers and getting to know the 'stage world'. My very first performance was in a huge hall where there were more than 300 people. I performed at Federation Square in Melbourne and met even more people. All this happened in just two to three months. After I finished my course at the English language school, I went to a college. I was extremely happy when I saw that they also had dance classes.

My performing life became even more intense and busy. I was giving one or two shows a week. I also had around 20 hours of practice a week – four at school, 16 at studios or outside with friends or by myself in the garage. One day I was asked to be in a magazine photo shoot. That was pretty amazing.

Everything seemed perfect, way too perfect. Later that week, we got a call from Romania. My grandma had died.

I felt so sad. I did not get a chance to talk to her or see her again, to tell her that I loved her and that I will not forget her. To say goodbye is so important.

My mum and stepdad flew to Romania for the funeral. I stayed behind because I couldn't miss school. Having time to myself meant that I could think about my future. On sleepless nights I asked myself: 'Do I want to become a dancer?'

The Unexpected Child

I know a lot of professional dancers. They teach classes and they get paid for it. They make a decent living. It's not much but it's what they love and they are happy. But I was not sure. I like to be the best dressed and to have the latest stuff. I didn't know if I could afford all that on a dancer's salary.

Slowly, I lost faith in myself. I stopped dancing for a few weeks. It felt wrong not to do what I loved best. But inside I was confused and muddled. Then I took part in an event where my favourite dance crew performed – the crew I used to watch on *America's Best Dance Crew* on Saturday nights!

I couldn't believe my eyes. Seeing them happy and dancing with passion was too much. I said to myself, 'This is what I want to do. It's going to be hard but hey, nothing is easy in life'.

Next day I was back giving 110 per cent on the dance floor. I learned some new moves and competed with other people. One day I got a call for a photo shoot. I was excited because this one was professional. They asked lots of questions and wrote about me in a newspaper. Then I hosted for Supafame, which is a big clothing line, and that's when my life started to really change. People recognised me on the street and asked for my autograph. It was amazing.

Life became very busy. I practised, worked at a pizza shop for pocket money, studied for my VCE, and performed. I was tired but that didn't stop me. Just as well, because a few months later, I met my greatest inspiration: Brian Puspos, the biggest hip-hop choreographer in the world.

I took one of his dance classes in Melbourne. Watching him work was incredible. He was only 19 and he was the best choreographer in the world.

'I could be like that in a few years time', I told myself.

Now if anyone asks me what do I want to do, I say that I want to become a professional dancer.

Life is amazing. It gives you lots of opportunities. You just need to take them at the right time and believe in yourself. Coming to Australia was definitely the best thing that happened to me.

The Key to Success
Nilofer Zafari

I came to Australia as a refugee when I was 12 years old. My grandfather and an uncle died during the war in Afghanistan. I belong to a large family. When we decided to leave, some had to stay behind. We have been separated since that day.

I often wished I could see my family again, enjoy being with them, and experience the depth of the love we shared. But I think those times are gone. All I know is that a person who does not have the love of his or her parents and siblings is poor indeed. Their love and support makes us strong. That is why I say that I am stronger than a rock that will never break.

After some years in Pakistan, my father travelled to Australia by boat. He sponsored the rest of the family and we came here in 2005. The family settled in Adelaide and I went to school, starting off in Year 6. We moved around a fair bit until I was in Year 9. Not to be deterred, I continued my studies till Year 12, studying Maths, ESL Studies, Dari (my own language), Biology and Research Project. My research project topic was earthquakes.

As you can imagine, it wasn't easy settling in to a new country and culture. People were so different and the lifestyle unlike anything I had experienced to that point. To put it simply, each and every thing was different and new. But I have adapted to the culture, language and way of life very well. You might say I have been working hard for a bright future.

This has been a learning experience for me and it has made me stronger. I am confident enough to handle more difficult times. If I had remained in Afghanistan or Pakistan, there is no way I would have had the chance to get a degree or to be a professional person. Australia is where I can satisfy my thirst for education.

If there is one thing I have learned, it is that change is a natural part of life. We must change our strategy to adapt to new situations. When something unexpected happens, I become positive and try to alter the way I think and approach my problems. I study hard and win awards. It's because I have an aim in mind. My high school studies are preparing

The Key to Success

me for a Health Science pathway at university. I hope to study Health Science, Food and Nutrition, Science or Business.

I was born in Afghanistan but Australia is my home. Western Australia is my favourite part of the country because it's big and beautiful.

A New Beginning

Research and Discussion

1   Why did Maisam's father leave Afghanistan? What was life like in Maisam's village when he was growing up? Discuss in class, giving examples from the story.

2   What are some of the differences between a student going to school in Australia and a student going to school in Afghanistan? Do you think everyone should have the right to an education, regardless of the country in which they are born? Explain with reasons and examples.

3   What did coming to Australia mean for Maisam and his family? How is this different from people who migrated legally to Australia from other countries?

Writing and Creating

1   Write a diary entry of the first day Maisam started school in Australia. Include all the possible emotions he would have felt as well as the difficulties in adapting to school life in Australia.

2   Be creative and retell Maisam's story from Rohollah's point of view. In your story, write about how you imagine he would have felt about moving to Australia.

3   Pretend you are Maisam and write a short story about the differences between life in Australia and Afghanistan. This can be a continuation from Maisam's original story.

The Unexpected Child

Research and Discussion

1   Why did Robert's mother change her mind about going through with her pregnancy? What was Robert's life like in Romania? Describe with examples from the story.

2   Was Robert a good dancer from an early age? Explain with reasons based on the information in the story.

3   What are your aspirations and dreams? Are these the same as what your parents or guardians think about your future? How important are your parents' views on your future? Explain with reasons.

4   What is the secret to Robert's success in dancing? What does this say about other migrants or refugees coming to live in Australia?

Writing and Creating

1   Write one thing Robert regretted since coming to Australia. Explain the reasons by giving examples from the story.

2   List the hard work Robert had to do and the challenges he faced in a table.

3   Write a feature article about Robert's future success in dancing, to be published in the newspaper 10 years from now. Use the information in the story and images or photos to help you with the article. Include a title, date and information on what separates Robert from other dancers.

4   Design a crossword puzzle for the story. Make up questions for *Across* and *Down*, using the information in the story.

The Key to Success

Research and Discussion

1   Why did Nilofer leave Afghanistan to go to Pakistan? How did she feel about leaving her home country?

2   According to Nilofer, education is 'The key to success'. Explain what she means by this. Do you think there are other important factors for success? Discuss this in class giving examples from the story.

3   What are some of the strategies Nilofer used to help her become successful and adapt easily to life in Australia? Do you have any strategies that you use when faced with difficult challenges or change in life?

4   Research and find information about a notable Australian who migrated to Australia from another country. Write a report about this person and present it to the class.

Writing and Creating

1   Write a paragraph describing Nilofer as the protagonist of the story, 'The Key to Success'. Use the adjectives 'optimistic', 'studious', 'independent' and 'persistent', supported with examples from the story in your sentences.

2   Work with a partner to design a poster titled 'Secrets of Success in English'. On your poster include step-by-step instructions and examples on ways to be successful in studying English this year.

3   Why do you think Australia is the ideal place for Nilofer to 'satisfy her thirst for education'? Write a short piece on why education is important to you.

Meeting Michael Jackson
Kobra Moradi

The plane landed at Sydney airport. Despite sitting near a window, she had a massive headache. It was her first time on a plane. Back in her village, she often heard unbelievable stories about a giant thing made out of metal. People said that it could fly with human beings in its belly. She did not believe the tales. It seemed like a lie – until she set foot in an aeroplane and started to fly. Almost immediately, she sensed freedom. As each minute passed, she felt that she was getting closer to safety and, more importantly, to her dad.

She stepped out of the plane, spread her arms like a bird, and took a massive gulp of Australian air. It tasted fresh and it felt welcoming. She looked at her big sister and said, 'There is nothing to be scared of. Even the air is friendly and safe'.

Safora waited at the airport with her family.

'There he is, sweetie', said her mother. 'That's your baba.'

Two men walked rapidly towards them. One was tall, with dark brown hair. He looked too young to be Safora's father. She looked at the other man and kept staring as the small bodies grew bigger and bigger as the men approached in the crowd.

The man with fair skin and grey hair had a big smile on his face. He pushed people out of the way as he jogged towards his family. He opened his arms to fit in all his children and they ran into his loving embrace. He was laughing and there were tears of joy running down his face.

After he kissed everyone on the cheek, it was Safora's turn to get her father's attention. She knew this man was her dad and yet she was shy. He kissed her and her heart started racing. She could not help it; she burst into tears.

Her father lifted her up and said, 'Sh, it is all right now. I am with you. Your baba is with you'.

The family made a big scene, embracing, kissing and crying. People stared at them. Safora did not care what they thought. It was a family reunion.

'Come on', her father said. 'You must be tired and hungry. Let's go.'

Temur, Safora's little brother, said, 'Where are we going?'

'We are going to my friend's house', replied his father.

'Why to your friend's house? Let's go to our house', Temur replied.

'We don't have a house yet, son. But we will be in our own house soon, and you can choose it.'

'Cool, I want a house with a pool so I can learn how to swim', said Temur excitedly.

'Okay, we will get a house with a pool.'

Temur walked away with a big smile on his face.

After two weeks the family travelled to Griffith by train. Safora's mother carried a basket of fruit and bread. She offered some to Safora, but Safora was too excited to eat.

'Mum, Zakia said that we can go to school. Is that true?'

'Yes darling, you can go to school', the mother replied.

'What year should I go into, Mum?'

'You will be in Grade 6.'

Now that Safora had her mother talking she wasn't going to give up. She wanted answers to all the questions she had stored in her head since the day she arrived in Sydney.

'When are you going to buy my books?'

'When you are enrolled in a school. Now eat something. I know you are hungry.'

Even though Safora did not want to eat the apple her mother held out, she bit a huge chunk and chewed contentedly. She closed her eyes and started to rewind her memory back to Hazarajat. She saw herself among her friends, sewing clothes for her doll while listening to her older sister and her friends sing a Hazaragi couplet:

Sare koye beland zardak namosha
Dele dokhtar da permardak namosha
Ke permardak jaye babe she mosha
Jawan bacha nor e dede she mosha

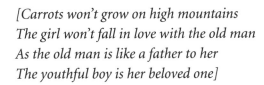

[Carrots won't grow on high mountains
The girl won't fall in love with the old man
As the old man is like a father to her
The youthful boy is her beloved one]

She saw herself take the sheep to the high mountain and go every morning to the river to get water for her mother. She pictured her beloved grandmother brushing her hair and giving her lollies from the corner of her big flowery scarf.

'When you go to Australia, make sure you don't forget your grandmother', the old woman said. 'Your grandmother will miss you, my darling. Try very hard at school. It will make me very happy. When you come back, I will give you lots of lollies.'

The words faded as Safora woke up to the loud horn of the train.

When she was in Hazarajat, the only celebrity everyone knew was Michael Jackson. He was a big idol for all the kids in the village. When Safora told them that she will see Michael Jackson in Australia she saw the jealousy in their eyes. All her friends said, 'Safora, please send us a CD of Michael Jackson and say hi to him from us'. She promised that she would.

They arrived in Griffith. After three weeks living with a family friend, they moved to a rented house of their own. Their father enrolled them at a school that was a mere 15 minutes walk from the house.

Safora was very excited and was running along the footpath.

'Wait for us, wait for us, Safora', shouted Temur.

'Quick, walk faster you guys', Safora shouted back.

'Wait, we are coming', her father laughed.

Safora ran back to her dad and her brother. She looked at her father and said, 'Baba, what if they don't let me into school because I am a girl?'

He smiled and took her hands. 'In Australia everyone can go to school.'

Safora was relieved. 'Great', she said. 'I can't wait. Let's walk faster.'

They made their way through the school gates. Safora looked around and couldn't believe her eyes. The school is too big, she thought. There

Meeting Michael Jackson

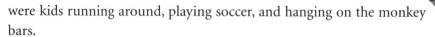

were kids running around, playing soccer, and hanging on the monkey bars.

'Come along', her father said.

In no time they were in the school office.

A woman with short black hair, tanned skin and dark brown eyes invited them to step into a small office.

The woman and Safora's dad exchanged a few words that Safora did not understand. Then the woman wrote on a paper and Safora's father signed. The woman smiled and shook hands with Safora's father as they left the room.

Safora was amazed at how quickly everything had happened.

'Is that it, Baba?' she asked.

'Yes, you can come to school from tomorrow.'

'But I don't have a uniform ...'

'That's all right. We will get it today,' her dad reassured her.

They made their way back home. Safora was happy. It had been the best day of her life. Australia had given her so much already and tomorrow she will make new friends.

As they turned into their street, Safora said in a soft voice, 'Australia is a new hope, Baba'.

A Place Where I Belong
Nazifa Reza

What was life like before?

Everything was different, from top to bottom.

I remember running away from home, just to be free with my friends. I felt more comfortable outside than staying indoors.

One day my friend and I just took off without telling anyone. We stayed away for about two hours and I missed my religious class, which was usually after lunchtime. I was worried because I never wanted my mum to get angry at me. When I came back, my mother screamed my name and asked where I was. I wanted to answer her question, but she was angry and wanted to hit me. She raised her hand to her cheeks and said, 'Don't ever do this to me again'. The weird thing is I wanted her to hit me so that I could learn a lesson. Later I found out she could never hurt anyone. She could not have slapped me or anyone else for that matter.

Compared to other families who had about 10 people in the one house, my family wasn't that big. My father had gone to Australia, so we lived with my uncle. He took care of us.

Life was pretty awesome. I was with my friends all the time, playing outside. When I finished with my religious classes I went out to play and didn't come home till dusk. My mum didn't restrict my brother and I, so long as we didn't get into trouble. 'Don't achieve something by choosing a bad path', she used to say. I understood what she meant and always tried to follow this rule.

I hated saying goodbye to my friends when we left Afghanistan. It was crazy because I was excited and upset at the same time. On the one hand, I wanted to be free. On the other hand, I knew I was never coming back. It was horrible.

We left early in the morning and arrived in Pakistan at night. During the trip, armed Taliban soldiers stopped the truck and searched everywhere. The truck dropped us off at my aunt's house. We stayed there for some weeks until we found a house of our own.

The family rented a house and started to live a different life. My brothers, sisters and I had to go to a place called the 'Centre', which is an English class, for two hours or so a day. We paid our fees once a month

and the teachers weren't strict compared to the teachers in Afghanistan, who sometimes hit you with a big stick. It was a new routine and we got used to it quickly. The only thing I didn't like was that I couldn't go outside much because of kidnappings and people gossiping.

On the way home from school, I used to take the backstreets because most of the kidnappings happened on the main street. I was pretty confident that I could take care of myself if something happened. One day, a guy opened the door to a house and said, 'Come in'. I was shocked and scared. I had no idea what he was talking about. He followed me for about five metres and then disappeared. I ran all the way home and never went back to that street again.

The months flew by. One day I realised we had lived in Pakistan for two years. My dad called often to see if we needed money or any special things that his brothers could get for us, but everything was fine. During one of his calls, Dad said that our visas had come through. We could go to Australia.

We spent the next month packing. My mother could see that I was upset. She said, 'I promise you that life will be better there. Don't worry. If you don't like it, you can always come back'.

What I couldn't tell her was that I didn't want to go to Australia. I just wanted to go back to my own country, where I felt like I could be myself.

But it wasn't her decision. Dad decided everything from Australia. The worst part was saying goodbye, knowing you probably would not see your friends and relatives again. It was really awful. By the end of it all I felt like I'd said enough goodbyes for one lifetime.

I was curious about sitting inside a plane. I wasn't much of a traveller and usually got carsick. But this was all right. I guess the anticipation of going to a new country stopped me from vomiting.

It had been 12 years since I'd seen my father. I hardly recognised him. But it was really good to see him waiting for us at the airport. We had dinner at his friend's house and then we drove to our house. Dad showed us new things so that we could be independent. He told Mum

that he missed us and a week later we went to school. My youngest sister and brother and I went to primary school; my older sister and brother went to high school.

My English wasn't bad. I started wearing a school uniform and eating different food and going to different places. Life changed. After a year I went to high school. I was lonely and uncomfortable there. I wanted to be more like Aussie students because they were always free from pressure. But somehow I couldn't quite manage it.

Just as I was settling in, we moved to Melbourne. That was a completely different kettle of fish. By this time my brothers and sisters could speak English, but Mum and Dad couldn't. They said it was too difficult. We translated for them.

I have lived in Australia for three years now. I am trying to build a new life here, but I never want to forget where I was born. One day, for sure, I want to go back and live with my friends and with my own people again. I appreciate what my identity is and the place that I belong. However, I will never be the same person I was back then.

A Place Where I Belong

My Journey to Happiness
Taiyeba Ansari

When you look into my eyes, you see a girl with dreams, desires and hopes for the future. When you look at my smile, you see a girl whose dreams have come true. It looks as if there is nothing wrong and she has all the happiness of today and tomorrow. In truth every smile has a million pains behind it.

I'm 18 years old and I'm a student in south-eastern Melbourne. I was born in Afghanistan and brought up there until the age of nine. Father put pressure on me to be the perfect child. I started religious school when I was four years old. When I was five I learned to read the Holy Qur'an in one month. When I turned six, my father sent me to a school that was 10 kilometres away from where I lived. He was rushing things and he worked extremely hard, but I never asked why.

My father came to Australia as an asylum seeker in 2000, right before my youngest brother was born. Father fled Afghanistan because of the war and the fact that he was an ex-soldier in the 1970s, fighting the Soviet Army. If he'd stayed on the Taliban would have killed him.

The night before he left, he came home late. Mother was worried about him. I could tell by looking into her eyes that she was hiding something. I put my hands in her lap and asked, 'Where is Father?'

She didn't say anything. Just stood up and walked around the room. There was a knock on the door and father came in. He looked terrible.

'Taliban', he yelled, as he ran into the back room with mother and hid the plastic bag he was carrying.

They talked into the night. Every word my father uttered made my mother cry. At one stage I heard her whimper, 'You are not coming back?'

Later that night, I found out that the plastic bag he had hidden so well was filled with borrowed money.

I can still remember the cold, gloomy morning when he left. I leaned against the front door of our house and watched him disappear into the fog. I remember the white Islamic cap on his head and the creamy shawl wrapped around him as he walked away. Seeing my mother cry as she watched him leave, I could not help but cry with her.

Mother grieved constantly and prayed to Allah to bring us news about my father. She started farming to provide food for us. By day she worked in the fields and by night she sewed, just so I could go to school. Most nights she went to bed without dinner. What little food there was went to her four children.

Five months passed. One day, Dad rang to say he had reached Australia. He had to remain in detention, he said, until he received his residency.

I continued to study, coming first in class and working hard to make something of myself. These dreams didn't last long. Everything came to a halt when I was diagnosed with severe depression. The doctor put me on medication and sent me home. I was often sick and stayed in bed for days. This went on for months – headaches, depression – it was ongoing. As I lay in bed I thought of what may have led me to this point.

I was often punished as a child, even for the smallest thing. I remember being treated very harshly by my teachers and parents, and by the age of eight I hated school so much that I hardly ever turned up to class. The physical scars have faded, but the pain is still inside me, burning day and night.

My father called every now and then. He was concerned about me and very encouraging, but it changed nothing. How can a mere phone call change anything when your every waking moment is filled with fear and violence and horrible poverty? How do you deal with that? It gave me nightmares so that I was afraid to fall asleep and afraid to wake up. There were times when I thought it would be better to disappear. I was so lost and felt that no one would even notice if I was gone. As far as I was concerned, there was no future ahead of me. I lived for the night and the thought of waking up to another tomorrow was unbearable.

After a while I started going to school again. In the morning, my mother made me say 'There is no god except Allah and Muhammad is the Messenger of Allah' three times before I left. I cried all the way to school, because leaving the house meant the end of the world.

My Journey to Happiness

Even so I continued to go to school and to help my mother around the house. I will never forget my little sister crying all night because there was nothing for her to eat. It was a living hell.

I was nine years old when my father got his permanent residency. The minute it came through, he asked a friend to illegally transport us to Pakistan. I was smuggled out disguised as a boy, with my head shaved, so that the Taliban wouldn't take me.

Life in Pakistan was worse than Afghanistan. There was limited education, poor sanitation, and lack of water. Consequently, my illness got worse. My mother had to pay lots of money for my medications because there was no healthcare.

My father brought us to Australia in 2005 and we were a family again. At first, Australia was like paradise. My health improved. I felt safer and I started to feel better about myself. I felt that there is no place like Australia and this is where I belong. In reality, that was far from the truth.

Like many migrants, I suppose, I felt lonely here. People laughed at me because I couldn't speak English. There was no one I could open my heart to, no one to laugh or cry with. It was very lonely and I had so much pain inside. It was almost killing me. What really broke my heart was when a white guy told me to get out of his country and go back to where I came from.

I got sick again. The only way to fight the depression was to fight against myself. I starved myself until my body started to shut down. I thought this was the only thing I could do to make myself feel better, but it made me feel worse.

I started studying ESL at high school. When I was 12, I decided to become a police officer. The police uniforms and cars inspired me and I was delighted to have such a goal. It gave me something to aim for and my health started to improve again. I moved to another high school when I was in Year 8 and discovered a talent for singing. My three best friends were very supportive.

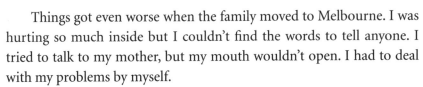

Things got even worse when the family moved to Melbourne. I was hurting so much inside but I couldn't find the words to tell anyone. I tried to talk to my mother, but my mouth wouldn't open. I had to deal with my problems by myself.

I started spending more and more time on my own in my room thinking of what I could do to make the pain go away. I thought about all my problems and felt so helpless and empty. I fell asleep thinking about the peace I would feel if I could just disappear.

A few days later, I was walking home with my sister and my friend when a white guy came over and pulled my hijab down, saying I was wearing my mother's tea towel. It offended me and broke the pride I had in me for being a Muslim girl.

I came to Australia so I could live a little longer than I expected, so that I can live a better life and educate myself, and this is what I get. A man pulling my hijab and telling me I was going to blow up a bomb. Didn't he know I wear my hijab because it shows my purity and my dignity? It's my religion and I obey it.

That night I cried myself to sleep. The next day, I decided to make a change in the world. I talked to the deputy principal at school and he suggested that I should talk about my experiences.

Together with another girl, I did a presentation about refugees who come to Australia in the hope of a better life. I made a difference at my school and God willing I will make a difference in my country too one day.

From that day on, I found an inner peace. I had been walking in darkness and suffering for so long I had not realised I had drifted away from who I really was – from Allah and from my dear family. They were almost strangers to me. I decided to begin my life anew. I decided to believe, live and return to Allah. My first step was to ask for forgiveness.

As time moved on, I became happier. My life became easier and better. The first sign I got from Allah was when I dreamed of Him on a holy night. I didn't see Him in my dreams, I didn't hear Him but I felt His presence.

My Journey to Happiness

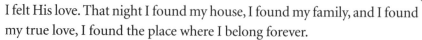

I felt His love. That night I found my house, I found my family, and I found my true love, I found the place where I belong forever.

In the morning I told my parents about the dream.

A few nights later I dreamed of the Prophet Muhammad on Judgement Day; I was with a sheikh in a dark place trying to find my way out. The sheikh asked me to write 'There is no god except Allah and Muhammad is the Messenger of Allah'. No matter how much I tried, I couldn't write it in Arabic. So I wrote it in English. A blinding light struck my face and from the brightness came the Prophet. I realised I was holding Imam Ali's sword in my hand.

From that night, I promised Allah I would never lose hope. I submitted myself completely to His will.

I began a new life filled with hope. The love of my family came back to me and I returned the love. I am finally happy and face whatever problems life presents with confidence.

I'm currently studying nursing. I want to get into medicine so that I can cure the hearts broken by the war and conflict. I'm also doing professional writing and editing so that I can write the stories of these broken people. I have also joined the Australian Defence Force. And some day I want to return to music and singing.

One day, I will make a difference in this world.

Meeting Michael Jackson

Research and Discussion

1   How did Safora feel when she met her dad for the first time at the airport? Describe using your own words.
2   Why does Safora want to go to school so much? How does she feel about her new home, Australia? Did her view change after she arrived in Australia? Provide examples from the story to support your answers.
3   What are the differences between Safora's new home and her old home? Do you believe Safora and her siblings will ever truly feel like they belong in Australia? Explain with examples.

Writing and Creating

1   Hazaragi is a dialect spoken by Hazara people in the region called Hazarajat in central Afghanistan. Explain the meaning of the Hazaragi couplet Safora's older sister and her friends sing in the story. Comment on the social and cultural values embedded in the song.
2   Draw a comic strip of the story using 8–10 frames. Some images could include Safora and her sister in the plane or Safora and her father meeting for the first time at Sydney Airport.
3   Write a diary entry as Safora at the end of her Year 12 formal in Australia. Include the differences on how you felt on your first day at school and now. Also comment on your feelings about identity and belonging as well as your plans for future life in Australia.
4   Explore the use of punctuation in the story. Find examples of the punctuation marks below. Write one example of each in your book and explain their function in creating meaning.
    a   Apostrophe:
        i   Contraction
        ii   Possession
    b   Quotation marks
    c   Colon

A Place Where I Belong

Research and Discussion

1   How was life in Pakistan compared to Afghanistan for Nazifa and her family? Did they feel safer in Pakistan? Why? Provide evidence from the story.
2   Nazifa and her family had to move to the neighbouring country Pakistan because of the violence caused by the Taliban. She says, 'I just wanted to go back to my own country, where I felt like I could be myself'. What does this sentence show about Nazifa's sense of identity and belonging at the time?
3   The places we live in and the people we meet shape who we are and to which groups we belong. Do you agree? Give examples from the story and your life to support your view on this.

Writing and Creating

1   When Nazifa was very late returning home after school she used the verb 'worry' to describe her feelings, saying 'I was worried because I never wanted my mum to get angry'. Find and make a list of similar verbs Nazifa used in her story to describe feelings.
2   Use these quotes from the story to answer the questions below:
   - 'I wanted to be more like Aussie students because they were always free from pressure.'
   - 'I just wanted to go back to my own country, where I felt like I could be myself.'
   - 'I appreciate what my identity is and the place that I belong.'

   a   Explain, in a sentence or two, what Nazifa means by each quote.
   b   Find the quotes in the story. Draw a timeline of the order in which the quotes appear.
   c   Each of the quotes represents a stage of Nazifa becoming an Australian. For example, the second quote is when Nazifa feels the need to negotiate between her culture and her traditions and the Australian culture and way of life. This can be called 'The Arrival' stage. Work with a partner to name and describe the other stages and fit the quotes into them, then explain your stages to the rest of the class.

d   Add another example sentence for each quote in a table you draw in your book.

3   Use one of the quotes from Question 2 as a title for a speech to be delivered at a school assembly OR a short story to enter in a writing competition for Year 7 and 8 students at your school.

My Journey to Happiness

Research and Discussion

1   Why was Taiyeba dressed as a boy and her head shaved on the way to Pakistan? What was her life like in Pakistan? Give examples.

2   Taiyeba thought 'there is no place like Australia and this is where I belong. But in reality Australia wasn't the place for me at all'. What does she mean by this? Did she feel she belonged to Australia at that time? Give examples from the story to support your answer.

3   Taiyeba had long suffered from severe depression and abuse in Afghanistan and this continued when she came to Australia. She felt unwelcome and rejected by the society that she was living in, causing her further pain at school and outside school. Does this behaviour of rejection have negative implications for both parties? What sort of disadvantages are there for a group that rejects rather than accepts someone new? Give examples from real life and from other groups such as in sport, family etc.

Writing and Creating

1   Using the relevant software and ICT tools, create a concept map of this story. Include the characters, places and themes in your concept map as well as important quotes.

2   Use your dictionary to find the meaning of the words 'adapting', 'appearance', 'culture shock', 'discrimination' and 'tolerance'. Write five sentences about identity and belonging using at least one of these words in each sentence. Discuss your sentences with others in your class.

3   Rewrite the story 'My Journey to Happiness' in reverse. Instead of Taiyeba, change the protagonist to an Australian girl named Chloe and write about her journey to happiness in Afghanistan. Include the details of her life in Afghanistan around the same time Taiyeba started living in Australia, as well as her feelings about her identity and belonging.

Appendix

Kpana Bolay migrated to Australia with her family from her home country of Liberia. She is 17 years old and currently attends Para Hills High School in Adelaide, South Australia. Along with her talent for writing stories, she also has a flair for poetry.

Melissa Miller is currently a student at Underdale High School in Adelaide and is from an English, Polish and New Zealand background. Her passions include singing, acting and writing. She has ambitions of becoming a renowned actress. Melissa uses writing to express her feelings and experiences in her life.

Fatima Moradi was born in Kabul, Afghanistan and migrated to Australia in 2005 when she was 11 years old. She spent most of her childhood travelling from Afghanistan to Pakistan. She finished secondary school in 2011 and is currently studying a Bachelor of International Business degree.

Jamila Shirzad is a student at Narre Warren South P-12 College in Melbourne's south-eastern suburbs. She is 16 years old and migrated to Australia from Afghanistan with her family at a young age. Her passions include reading fantasy books and when she is older she would like to help people by becoming a psychologist.

Kobra Moradi attends Hallam Senior College in Melbourne. She migrated to Australia at the age of 10 with her family. She is currently in Year 11 and hopes to attend university and study political science or international studies. Her passion is travelling and she hopes to one day work with a humanitarian organisation such as the United Nations.

Syed Hussain Mosawi attends Narre Warren South P-12 College in Melbourne's south-eastern suburbs. He migrated to Australia at the age of 15 by himself and is currently in Year 12. He hopes to study a Bachelor of Science at university. His passions include writing and scientific research.

Jaweed Rahimi attends Narre Warren South P-12 College in Melbourne. He migrated to Australia with his sisters in 2010 at the age of 17. He is currently in Year 11 and completing a Certificate III course in VFA Fitness. When he gets his Australian citizenship, he hopes to attend the Australian Defence Force Academy.

Mohammad Mohsim Jafari is currently in Year 11 at Narre Warren South P-12 College in Melbourne. He left his home country and took refuge in Australia at the age of 16. His dream is to study a civil engineering course at university and help create buildings and infrastructure. His passions include writing and he hopes one day to be a well-known lawyer as well as a civil engineer.

Sayed Hayatullah Mosawi attends Holroyd High School in Sydney's western suburbs. He migrated to Australia in 2010 at the age of 15. In the future, he wants to study medicine at university. His dream is to become a great doctor and help people.

Izel Öztürk attends Findon High School in Adelaide. She is 15 years old and is currently in Year 11. She was born in Turkey and migrated to Australia in 2006. Her passions include writing and soccer and she hopes to attend university and get a law degree.

Zahra Ali is 16 years old and attends Findon High School. She migrated from Afghanistan in 2007 with her family at the age of 11. She hopes to attend university and study a Bachelor of Psychology. Along with her passion for writing, she also enjoys dancing and cooking.

Blaise Mupenzi David is 15 years old and currently attends Underdale High School in Adelaide, South Australia. After spending some time in the Kyangwali Refugee Camp in Uganda, he discovered his love for soccer and now plays for a soccer club in Adelaide. His dream is to play for an English soccer team like Manchester United.

Roshan Jafari attends Narre Warren South P-12 College and is currently in Year 11. She migrated to Australia at the age of 13 and hopes to study law at university. Her passions are writing stories about her hopes and dreams, and she would like one day to help disadvantaged people all over the world. Her motto is, 'Always be supportive and help each other. You only have one life so enjoy it with happiness'.

Azaara Perakath is currently a Year 11 student at Glenunga International High School in Adelaide. She migrated to Australia at the age of 16, leaving behind vibrant Hong Kong. Unlike the creative ideas that seem to flow when putting pen to paper, she is quite indecisive about a potential career. However, she is passionate about writing and enjoys debating and might study law at university.

Robert Matyus attends Narre Warren South P-12 College. He migrated to Australia at the age of 15 with his mother and is currently in Year 11. He hopes to achieve a good VCE score to further his studies at university. His passions include dancing and working out.

Nilofer Zafari lives in Adelaide, South Australia. She completed Year 12 in 2011. She is currently studying Software Engineering at the University of South Australia. She migrated to Australia in 2005 with her family and hopes to finish her studies and become a good engineer.

Maisam Haidari attends Narre Warren South P-12 College in Melbourne's south-eastern suburbs. He immigrated to Australia at the age of nine with his family, and is currently living in Melbourne with his brothers and sister. He hopes to study medicine at university and become a doctor.

Nazifa Reza attends Narre Warren South P-12 College and is currently in Year 12. She was born in Afghanistan and migrated to Australia in 2006 with her family. She moved to Melbourne in 2008. Her passion is writing and she hopes to become a web developer.

Taiyeba Ansari is from Melbourne's south-eastern suburbs and attended Narre Warren South P-12 College. She has since graduated and is currently attending university where she is studying to become a nurse.

She has also joined the Australian Defence Force where she hopes to make a difference in this world.

Dede Putra (illustrator) came to New Zealand from Indonesia in 2003 to further his studies in illustration. Since graduating from Auckland University of Technology, he has worked as an illustrator for children's and young adult books and some graphic novel projects. He has also worked as a concept artist and illustrator in the video games industry. He is currently working with Watermark, an Auckland-based group of illustrators.